"Will...[...]...ining her on t[...]..."

Suzanne studied him, and even in the pale light from the candles, he could see that her cheeks were rosy with excitement. "You'll more than do," she said in that smoky voice. Then her lips curved. "You'll do...me."

Greg's heart raced as he returned that saucy smile. "I sure will, sweetheart." Then, giving her a questioning look, he picked up a strand of tinsel. "Only, you seem to be covered in silver...."

"You wouldn't let me put icicles on the tree, so—"

"I like them much better here." He captured several stands lying across the swell of her breast and drew them back and forth over her bare skin. Then he leaned down and ran his tongue along the edge of her bra.

"That tickles." Suzanne's skin grew warm and flushed, and she began to quiver beneath him. "The icicles were a little joke," she said breathlessly. "I didn't realize it would feel like...this...when you took them off."

"It feels good, then?" he asked, picking icicles from her garter belt and dipping his tongue into her navel.

"Only one thing could feel better," she said, drawing him down to her. "And I can't wait until Christmas to experience it...."

Dear Reader,

Don't you love this time of year? Holiday spirits rise as temperatures dip (yes, even in Arizona) and we can find so many interesting ways to keep warm. I don't know about you, but I think the words *snuggle* and *cuddle* were invented for nights like these. When the cold wind blows, you have a perfect excuse to lure that man of yours over to the fire, or under a goose-down comforter. After all, you wouldn't want the poor guy to catch a chill.

And once you have him where you want him, may I recommend a little Temptation Heat? I guarantee that the blaze created in these pages by Greg and Suzanne will warm him up faster than any snifter of brandy or cup of hot chocolate. As bedtime stores go, *The Nights Before Christmas* isn't the sort to lull your sweetie to sleep. But that's not the idea, now, is it?

Happy Holiday Nights,

Vicki Lewis Thompson

Books by Vicki Lewis Thompson

Vicki Lewis Thompson
THE NIGHTS
BEFORE CHRISTMAS

HARLEQUIN®

TORONTO • NEW YORK • LONDON
AMSTERDAM • PARIS • SYDNEY • HAMBURG
STOCKHOLM • ATHENS • TOKYO • MILAN • MADRID
PRAGUE • WARSAW • BUDAPEST • AUCKLAND

This book is dedicated
to all the mothers and daughters, sisters and aunts
who make the holidays happen. You deserve a nice,
hot love story and a few hours to savor it.
Take a break!

ISBN 0-373-25953-0

THE NIGHTS BEFORE CHRISTMAS

Copyright © 2001 by Vicki Lewis Thompson.

All rights reserved. Except for use in any review, the reproduction or
utilization of this work in whole or in part in any form by any electronic,
mechanical or other means, now known or hereafter invented, including
xerography, photocopying and recording, or in any information storage
or retrieval system, is forbidden without the written permission of the
publisher, Harlequin Enterprises Limited, 225 Duncan Mill Road,
Don Mills, Ontario, Canada M3B 3K9.

All characters in this book have no existence outside the imagination of
the author and have no relation whatsoever to anyone bearing the same
name or names. They are not even distantly inspired by any individual
known or unknown to the author, and all incidents are pure invention.

This edition published by arrangement with Harlequin Books S.A.

® and TM are trademarks of the publisher. Trademarks indicated with
® are registered in the United States Patent and Trademark Office, the
Canadian Trade Marks Office and in other countries.

Visit us at www.eHarlequin.com

Printed in U.S.A.

"Suzanne, you need a rebound guy." Terri Edwards took a swig from her water bottle without breaking stride on the treadmill next to Suzanne's. She was in fabulous shape, which allowed her to converse normally.

Suzanne definitely could not converse normally, and holding her water bottle was out of the question. She could barely stay upright on the relentless monster, let alone form sentences. "A...rebound...guy?" She'd never have guessed a treadmill could be such a challenge, or that weight-lifting machines could be so...heavy.

The gym had looked impressive when she walked in, with its bright lights, cheery colors and the aroma of good honest sweat coming from dedicated folks wearing spandex and headbands. Besides, they'd had the cutest Christmas tree sitting on the sign-in desk. Suzanne had no idea where they'd found miniature barbells and jogging shoes for the decorations, but she'd been captivated. To top it off, her favorite Christmas song, "Carol of the Bells," had poured from the sound system, right on cue.

She'd taken it as a sign, and with Terri's encouragement, she'd put her name and her Visa card on the dotted line. Joining a health club had seemed like a good idea an hour ago. Exercise lifted the spirits, or so she'd heard.

"A rebound guy," Terri repeated. "Great body, not into commitment, somebody you wouldn't think of dating under normal circumstances. With a guy like that in your life for a few weeks, you'll soon be over Jared."

"I am...over Jared." She tripped and grabbed onto the rail for dear life. "I just...have...too much...free time."

Terri glanced at her. "You're walking on a slant there, babe. Pretty soon you'll be horizontal. Better get your feet under you."

"Right." She gritted her teeth and scrambled to catch up with the moving belt. Then she went too far and had to backpedal so she wouldn't fall on her butt.

"Let's take five." Terri leaned over and turned off Suzanne's treadmill.

"Thank you." Suzanne hung on the rail and panted as the sound system belted out "Jingle Bell Rock." The unrelenting cheer was getting on her nerves. "Thank you for saving my life." She gazed over at Terri. "Did I ever tell you I hate escalators, too? And those moving sidewalks at O'Hare give me hives. I'm not cut out for the gym, Terri. Nice thought, but I'm ready to retire my spandex and take up stamp collecting."

"Nonsense. It's your first day. Besides, you're already paid up for a year. Come on, we'll get something at the juice bar and then take a turn on the stair-climbers."

The juice bar sounded excellent. A real honest-to-goodness bar sounded even better. Hot coffee laced with Baileys and she'd be a happy woman. She stepped off the treadmill with caution, but even so, the ground seemed to be moving when she tried to walk.

"You forgot your water bottle and your towel." Terri draped the towel around Suzanne's neck and put the water bottle in her hand before guiding her over to a stool at the juice bar. "I guess you weren't kidding when you said you'd never been in a gym before."

Suzanne shook her head. "Nope, wasn't kidding."

"How do you keep from getting fat? No, don't answer that. You're one of those high-metabolism types I love to hate, and I don't even want to hear about it."

"I guess." Suzanne eased onto the stool. Her whole body still vibrated.

"I ate two rum balls at the office Christmas party last night, and if I don't put in an extra ten minutes on the stairclimbers, those rum balls will go straight to my hips." Terri hopped on the stool next to Suzanne's. "Get the mango-strawberry madness. It's terrific."

Suzanne ordered the mango-strawberry madness, and discovered it wasn't bad, but a Baileys and coffee would have been ten times better. She tried not to think of the money she'd shelled out for a year's membership at this torture club. She planned to spend two days downstate with her mother over Christmas, which was three weeks away. She hadn't been looking forward to the visit, but now it gave her a legitimate excuse to skip an evening at the gym.

Terri patted her arm. "Don't worry. You'll get into the swing of it. And even if you don't need the exercise to lose weight, you'll feel tons better once you're used to moving your body more. Deep breathing does so much for stress and anxiety, believe me. Desk jobs are not good for our health."

"Being in this gym with all these machines *produces* stress and anxiety in me," Suzanne said. "Maybe I'll get back into coin collecting. I used to love that as a kid. Somewhere in my storage unit I should still have the—"

Terri groaned and dropped her head to the counter.

"What? I'm talking about a perfectly acceptable hobby here. Lots of people are into it these days, with the new quarters coming out. In fact, I've even started saving them."

Raising her head, Terri gazed at Suzanne. "You do not need a hobby. You need a man."

Sure enough, the concept made her stomach tighten, as it had ever since Jared's departure. "I'll get one of those, too, sooner or later. Right now I'd rather look for quarters."

"How will you ever get a man at the rate you're going? It's been six months, and you refuse to let anybody fix you up. More than that, you walk around with this do-not-touch attitude that would warn off any guy but the terminally obtuse. I say you're gun-shy."

Suzanne opened her mouth to object.

"I don't blame you," Terri continued. "Jared wasn't very sensitive about the breakup."

"If you're referring to his comment that I'm an anal-retentive ice queen, I guess you could say that." Suzanne had taught herself to repeat the phrase with a smile to show that she wasn't bothered by it anymore. Which, of course, she was.

"That comment only reveals Jared's insecurities," Terri said.

"Absolutely." And hers, she thought. In the year she was with Jared she'd never been able to get into his rhythm. Her struggle to keep up with Jared's expectations had been a lot like trying to keep up with the treadmill tonight. Jared belonged to a gym like this one. He liked loud parties, action-adventure movies and marathon sex.

They'd never been right for each other, but he'd convinced her that they would be once she learned to loosen up. She'd never learned. Having him gone was a relief, which told her that she'd never really loved him, just the idea of being in love.

But she missed little things, like the scent of his aftershave in the bathroom, the rumble of male laughter, the comfort of cuddling on the couch. Jared hadn't been much for that, but he'd managed it on a few rainy afternoons.

Terri stirred her rosy drink with a straw. When she spoke, her tone was careful. "Have you ever heard anybody in our apartment building mention Greg?"

"The handyman? What kind of mention?"

"I mean, like, *mention.*"

"Uh, no." Whenever she thought of the handyman, she always felt a thrill of forbidden pleasure. Her first glimpse of him shortly after moving in had sent a jolt of sexual awareness through her. She'd never had that kind of reaction to a man before.

Since then she indulged in a secret fantasy life with Greg, and that was so unlike her. Even when she'd become involved with Jared, she'd sometimes pretended that he was Greg. She'd had more than one X-rated dream about him, and lately they'd become more frequent. But she had no intention of acting on those dreams. She wasn't the type to make the first move.

"You think I should go out with the handyman?" As if she could work up the nerve to ask him. Not in a million years.

"Not go *out*, exactly." Terri studied her. Then she lowered her voice. "You have to promise to keep what I tell you absolutely confidential. Greg's a nice guy, and he'd lose his job if his boss heard about it."

"Heard about what?" A shiver of anticipation ran through her. Her latest dream had been the hottest one yet. They'd been in the shower...

"Remember when I had that nasty breakup with Lenny?"

Suzanne brought her attention back to the conversation. "Look, I agree you bounced back from that faster than I'm recovering from Jared, but it's not the same—"

"I have Greg to thank for that miraculous rebound," Terri said.

"You do?" The shiver became a delicious tingle in her belly. She'd assumed that Greg had a girlfriend. Anybody that good-looking was bound to be taken.

"Keep your voice down." Terri leaned closer. "Jennifer, up in 24C, let me in on the secret. It seems that Greg specializes in mending the broken hearts of the career girls in our building."

"You mean...?" So he wasn't taken. Instead, he was something of a Casanova, which was disappointing. He looked more like a one-woman kind of guy. In her dreams, he'd vowed to love only her.

"I certainly do mean," Terri said. "He's great, Suzanne. The perfect rebound man. He's gorgeous and understanding, plus he knows a relationship will never go anywhere considering the big difference in lifestyles. He seems to like it that way."

"That's totally amazing." She would never have the courage to take advantage of the situation and go to bed with Greg, of course. A man with that much experience would intimidate the heck out of her. But knowing about his extracurricular activities put a whole new spin on her fantasies about him. Obviously he wasn't her secret soul mate, which had been a girlish idea in the first place. "It's like an urban legend or something."

"I know. There's a kind of sisterhood in the building, and we're all sworn to silence, to protect Greg's job. By telling you, I'm letting you into that sisterhood, and you must never, ever say anything unless you're absolutely sure that you've found another woman in our complex who needs Greg's services, someone you consider to be completely trustworthy."

"I understand. And thanks for trusting me that much."

"I do, or I wouldn't have said anything. But you have to approach Greg and make it clear that you won't put his job in jeopardy. He will never make the first move, which is understandable. The usual procedure is to ask him to fix something in your apartment, and while he's there, you begin talking about your breakup. He'll take it from there."

"I can't imagine."

"Can't you? Don't tell me you haven't noticed the body on that man."

Suzanne blushed. "Oh, I can imagine *that*." Actually, her dreams were very explicit, giving her the shape and size of Greg's considerable endowments. "I can't imagine making the first move with him, I mean. Initiating the contact. That's not my strong suit, anyway, and in this case, I barely know the guy." And he was way different from what she'd thought.

"That's the beauty of it." Terri shoved her empty drink aside. "We're not talking about anything long-term, anyway. A quick repair, and you're on your way."

"No, I couldn't." It sounded somewhat shallow, yet thrillingly naughty, too. But sexual flings weren't her style. Fantasies were one thing, but turning them into reality led to heartache, like her parents' divorce.

"You don't know what you're missing," Terri said. "Think about it. This has been going on for at least two or three years, which means Greg's had an intensive course in how to patch up a girl's ego."

Not to mention his extensive experience in making the rest of her hum like a top. The concept turned Suzanne on, whether she wanted to admit it or not.

"You'll never hear Greg saying that someone's an anal-retentive ice queen," Terri continued. "I'll vouch for the fact that he's incredibly romantic. I'm guessing he was before, but after hearing about the crummy things guys say and do, he *really* knows what makes women happy."

Suzanne looked at her friend with her perky blond ponytail and her red and purple workout clothes. Terri was a take-charge woman if she'd ever seen one. Suzanne, on the other hand, let things come to her. She had to admit that some of the things that came to her weren't always terrific, like Jared, for example. He'd initiated the relationship, probably because of his egotistic belief that he could change her into a sex kitten.

"It's a good idea, Suzanne," Terri said.

"You know, I can picture you following through with this, because you go after what you want. But I'm—I'm not that good at putting myself out there."

Terri gazed at her. "I know, sweetie. That's partly why I suggested the gym. There's nothing passive about it."

"You are so right, and look at me! I'm miserable, a fish out of water. I don't think this is a quick fix, Terri. I've been a cautious type for a long, long time, which explains why I'm a financial analyst instead of in the sales division with you. But it was great of you to trust me with the information. I promise the secret is safe with me."

"Listen, you need to break your pattern and latch onto this. You really—"

"Let's try the stair-climbers." It was a radical way to end the conversation, considering how much she dreaded the stair-climbers, but another round on one of Terri's beloved exercise machines might be the only way they'd table the discussion of Greg, the rebound man.

SUZANNE MANAGED to survive the stair-climbers and the rowing machine, although her muscles had a little chat with her and promised to punish her for this craziness later. Terri didn't bring up the subject of Greg again until they walked into the lobby of their apartment building.

In the past, Suzanne had felt reassured whenever she walked into the redbrick complex. Its sturdy, Midwestern architecture and its location near Northwestern University appealed to her more than some of the glass and steel apartments out by Lake Michigan.

The lobby contained live plants instead of silk, and this time of year, a fresh Christmas tree filled the small area with the scent of pine. The lobby furniture reminded her of the upholstered pieces her parents used to have when she was a kid, before the divorce, back when life had been safe. She'd rented an apartment here because it felt secure, but now that she knew about Greg, that sense of homey security had vanished. In its place was a disturbing undercurrent of unbridled sensuality.

The idea of unbridled sensuality had always made her nervous. She always assumed that was what had led her father to take up with his young secretary, thus destroying life as Suzanne and her brother, Bill, had known it.

"Have you given any more thought to what we talked about?" Terri said as they stepped into the elevator.

"No," Suzanne said. That was a lie. Whenever she hadn't been reviewing the damage she was doing to her poor body, she'd been thinking about Greg and his fascinating sideline.

"You're doing yourself a disservice if you don't check him out."

"I'll think about it," she said, more to keep Terri quiet than anything. She had no intention of following through on this hot tip. She'd love to wipe her brain free of the whole concept, but that didn't seem likely, not when this was the most bizarre factoid she'd been given in quite a while.

Before Terri could continue her infomercial for Greg, the elevator stopped at the third floor and Suzanne got off, gym bag in hand. "See you in the morning, assuming I can still walk."

"You'll be fine. Soak in those herbal bath salts I gave you for your birthday."

"I will." Once the elevator door closed, Suzanne allowed herself to sag a little. That workout had been murder, and she no more wanted to go back to the gym in two days than row around Lake Michigan in a dinghy. Come to think of it, rowing around the lake might be easier, even taking into consideration the iced-over parts. And she'd paid good money for this gym madness, which made no sense at all.

But she would go back, because once someone had pushed her into an activity the way Terri had with this gym caper, Suzanne tended to hang in for the duration. She might not be much of a self-starter, but once she got going, she was no quitter.

Soaking in the herbal bath salts was an excellent suggestion, though. She opened her apartment door and locked it carefully behind her. The apartment was as tidy as she'd left it. During her Jared period that rarely had been the case. Besides tossing his things around in a helter-skelter way, a trait she'd struggled to accept, he'd made fun of her Virgo tendency to want everything neat. Now that he was gone and the effects of his overwhelming personality had faded enough to give her some perspective, she realized that his comments had hurt her. Besides, it *was* her apartment, and she liked being able to find things.

Jared, whose parents were still married, didn't understand how order comforted her. Her parents' divorce had been messy, with many terrible arguments. Ten years later, her mother still felt a lot of resentment. Suzanne hadn't been able to tidy up any of that, but she could at least keep her surroundings peaceful. To that end, she'd worked hard to decorate this one-bedroom nest of hers. The white-on-white design scheme worked best when it was uncluttered. Her single accent of color was a red velvet pillow set on a diagonal in the middle of her ivory couch.

The color scheme also worked with her Christmas decorations. For several years she'd waged a quiet battle to reclaim the joy she used to feel during the holidays. She hadn't quite captured it yet, but she wasn't about to give up.

A three-foot tree sat in a corner on a skirted table. She'd considered white lights and white decorations to go with her furniture, but in the end she'd used multicolored lights and ornaments, much like the ones her parents used when she was growing up. The carved nativity scene on top of her TV cabinet was new this year. She had no idea what had happened to the one her parents used to have, but because her mother got teary-eyed whenever Suzanne brought it up she'd settled for one that resembled the old version she remembered.

She'd also won a poinsettia at the office Christmas party, and it looked festive on her coffee table. The room had a holiday feel, although nothing like her parents' house used to be this time of year. These days her mother had to be coaxed to even put up a tree.

Still carrying her gym bag, Suzanne walked back to the bedroom. She couldn't remember ever being quite this tired, but soaking in the tub might keep her from waking up crippled in the morning. Although her movements were slow, eventually she stripped down and had water running in the tub.

Then she opened the cabinet under the sink to take out the jar of bath salts. The jar sat in a puddle of water.

She stared at the puddle for several seconds while the

water continued to thunder into the tub. Surely the universe didn't work this way. But a steady drip from the U-joint under the sink told her otherwise.

Taking a towel from the rack, she tucked it under the drip. That would do for now. If she changed the towel regularly, she could put off the inevitable for a few days. But she wasn't the kind of person who could tolerate a dripping pipe for very long.

Not tonight, maybe not even tomorrow night, but eventually she'd need to call the handyman.

WHEN SUZANNE TALBOT CALLED about the leak under her bathroom sink, Greg's pulse leaped. He'd had a secret yen for the woman in 36C every since he passed her in the hallway about eighteen months ago. Since then he'd been keenly aware of her whenever they happened to be in the same vicinity.

He'd developed a fascination for the way her mahogany-colored hair curled at the slightest hint of dampness in the air. She usually tried to tame it with a bow, a clip or a scrunchie, but a few times he'd seen it rippling down to her shoulders, and the sight had made him catch his breath.

The same conservative streak that caused her to imprison her hair seemed to rule her choice in clothes. Although she had a lush figure, he'd only discovered that by strategic observation. During the work week she wore business suits in neutral colors, favoring black. And on weekends her outfits were often baggy sweats and oversize shirts. She seemed determined to minimize her sex appeal.

That only made her more intriguing to Greg. When he'd finally had a chance to look into her eyes one day, he'd been hooked. He'd always been partial to blue eyes and Suzanne's were Siamese-cat blue. But it was the intelligence shining from those eyes that nearly made him break his rule never to date someone living in this building.

Then the stockbroker, Jared, had come on the scene, saving Greg from making that mistake. Reason had prevailed. He couldn't afford to let himself care more than superficially about any of the single women who lived here. They were all career types with what must be high-paying jobs in order for them to afford the rent.

Talking to them and counseling them about their love lives was risky enough. Yet he hated to give up the satisfaction he got from bolstering their self-esteem after their overpaid, overeducated boyfriends had screwed up the relationship. That didn't mean he had any intention of taking it beyond friendship. He wasn't about to get physical with these women, even though a few had come on to him.

Sure, they might want fun and games now, and they certainly tempted him, but he'd been able to put aside the physical attraction and listen carefully to what they said. *Very* carefully. By listening, he inevitably learned that these career-minded women would never settle for a handyman with no college education. In the end they'd either dump him the way Amelia had, or they'd try to fix him. He was not changing his lifestyle to suit someone else, not when he'd made peace with his demons and liked the path he'd chosen. Even someone like Suzanne Talbot, who seemed to be everything he'd ever wanted in a woman, wasn't enough of a reward for him to give up the identity he'd carved out for himself.

Keeping that thought firmly in mind, he picked up the heavy wooden toolbox he'd inherited after his father died and climbed the fire stairs to the third floor. Shoot, he was such a maverick that he didn't even like elevators. A guy couldn't get very far in the corporate world if he didn't like riding in elevators. Most of the cushy jobs were on the top floor, and climbing the stairs would leave sweat stains on the Armani.

When he thought of it that way, he was able to see that Amelia had done him a favor by dumping him when he'd decided to leave college and give his savings to his widowed mother. If Amelia had stuck with him, he probably would have worked his tail off to earn more money and go back to school so he could be part of her world. He'd be in the rat race for sure by now. The thought made him shudder.

He might have ended up like Jared, perish the thought, with a cell phone constantly at his ear and self-importance that wouldn't quit. Fate hadn't seen fit to give him a lot of material possessions, and along the way he'd discovered they weren't important to him, anyway.

Greg didn't keep track of all the comings and goings in the building, but he made a point of knowing what was up with Suzanne. He'd become aware soon after the fact that her stockbroker boyfriend wasn't around anymore. A guy like that was hard to miss when he showed up, so the place was decidedly quieter without him. Cell phones and self-importance aside, Greg hadn't liked the way Jared had seemed to intimidate Suzanne.

Plus, he seemed unable to laugh at himself, which Greg thought was a major failing, especially for a woman like Suzanne who appeared to be very sensitive. Greg had been summoned one Saturday when Jared had gone for a jog and locked himself out while Suzanne was at the grocery store. Somehow the jerk had managed to blame Suzanne for the problem.

With the overbearing stockbroker gone, Greg figured Suzanne was better off. But she might be feeling blue, and she *was* good friends with Terri, so Terri had probably suggested she talk with him.

Which was okay. He enjoyed the mental stimulation. The flirting was okay, too. Terri was one of the women who'd kissed him, and he'd kissed back. A guy couldn't be blamed for enjoying a kiss now and then. But in Terri's case, as in every case, he'd gently eased away from taking the relationship any further.

Although he told himself to stay cool, Greg rang Suzanne's doorbell with keen anticipation.

2

GREG NOTICED RIGHT AWAY that Suzanne hadn't changed
into something more comfortable in honor of his arrival.
She was still in full business dress, wearing her black suede
suit like a coat of armor. A black velvet bow held her mahogany-colored hair back in a no-nonsense style.

There wasn't a single casual thing about her as she stood
in the doorway of her apartment. She'd even left on her
black pumps, something he thought most women kicked
off the minute they walked through the door. He wondered if she had an appointment somewhere. Maybe she
didn't intend to stay here and pour her heart out, after all.
Maybe her sink really had sprung a leak.

The disappointment he felt was another warning—he
should be very careful with this one. "Do you need to leave
soon?" he asked. "Because I can fix the leak while you're
gone." He grinned at her in an attempt to ease the lines of
anxiety in her expression. "You don't have to worry about
the silverware. I'm bonded."

"Uh, no, I don't need to go anywhere." Without returning his smile, she stepped away from the door. "Come in."

"You looked so together, I thought you might be on your
way out."

"Not really."

"Good." So they'd talk. Just talk. Kissing Suzanne would
be far more dangerous than kissing Terri had been.

He walked into the room and registered the white-on-white decor. She hadn't needed anything repaired since she'd moved in, so other than a brief glimpse when he'd let the stockbroker in that Saturday about six months ago, he'd had no idea how she'd fixed up the place.

The scent of pine drew his attention to the corner where her little tree twinkled. Because he'd pegged her as an orderly person, he wasn't surprised that the strings of lights and ornaments were hung in perfect symmetry. He pictured her squinting at the finished product to make sure that there were no bald spots or color clashes.

"I like your tree." He gave her another smile.

"Thanks." This time she smiled back, but she still looked very nervous.

He was impressed that she had a tree at all, though, considering that last Christmas she'd been part of a couple and this year she was alone. Apparently she wasn't about to let that stop her from celebrating, and he was glad to discover that. Her perky little evergreen shone like a badge of courage in the corner of her living room.

He'd expected the place to be immaculate, and it was. The red pillow sitting in the middle of her white sofa was fascinating, though. From the psychology texts he'd read, that pillow in the middle of all the virginal white said something about her sexuality. An erotic nature might be hiding under the sensible surface.

But he wasn't here to uncover her erotic nature. First he'd tighten the pipe connection that she probably loosened on purpose, and then he'd listen to her complain about her ex-boyfriend. Maybe he'd suggest ordering up some Chinese food. He'd be a shoulder for her to cry on—figuratively in this case—reassuring her that she was too good for the chump who'd left her.

Still, her appearance threw him. She didn't look like a woman about to let her hair down.

"The pipe's been leaking for three days." She led the way toward the bathroom. "This is the first chance I've had to call you."

Another unexpected comment. She didn't strike him as the type to make up a story about a pipe that had been leaking for three days. That was carrying the charade a little too far. But maybe she had more imagination than the other women he'd dealt with. Or maybe she loosened the pipe, lost her nerve and then had to spend three days working up to the call.

If so, then he'd enjoy helping her rebuild her confidence. Platonically, of course. Always platonically.

In order to get to the bathroom, he had to walk through her bedroom. It was very girly, with rose-printed fabric covering the quilt, armchair and curtains in shades of red and pink. But there, nestled against the pillows, was the devil himself.

He was a cute little doll dressed in bright red velvet, with a mischievous grin on his face and The Devil Made Me Do It written across his chest. Uh-*huh*. As he'd suspected from his first glimpse of Suzanne, still waters ran deep.

Her bedroom held the subtle scent of roses, but her bathroom was drenched in it. When he walked in, he was bombarded with an image of Suzanne, naked, spritzing the perfume in strategic places. The Devil Made Me Do It. The devil was having a field day with him right now, thumbing his nose at all those platonic vows Greg had taken.

Trying to calm his libido, he crouched in front of the cabinet under the sink and opened the oak doors. A steady drip had made a round spot on the pink towel she'd laid under the pipe. There was nothing erotic about that spot, and yet his mind leaped from damp towels to the image of

Suzanne stepping out of a steamy shower, glistening and wet.

He could assume that Suzanne had called him because she needed a shoulder to cry on. He'd known she was shy, so meeting him in full career-dress mode made sense, now that he thought about it. Suzanne wouldn't be the sort to let down her guard easily, but he had a knack for helping women open up and confide in him.

Assuming he used that talent with Suzanne, he wondered how well he'd be able to control himself once she opened up to him and became soft and vulnerable. He wondered if he'd be able to ignore the implications of that red pillow and that suggestive doll in the middle of her bed. He wondered how much trouble he could get into if he ignored the implications, if he broke all his rules, followed his instincts and took this fascinating woman to bed.

A lot of trouble, no doubt. But this time it might be worth the risk.

"Is it a bigger problem than I thought?" Suzanne asked from the bathroom doorway.

"No." He cleared the huskiness from his throat. "Minor stuff, it looks like." He got to his knees and fumbled with the latch on his toolbox. After getting it open with far more awkwardness than usual, he took out a small flashlight and beamed it up toward the source of the leak. That's when he found the rust that was causing it.

Suzanne certainly hadn't rusted the pipe. Much as he hated to admit it, she hadn't booby-trapped her sink in order to lure him into her apartment. Her call had been legitimate.

Damn.

THE MINUTE GREG STEPPED into her apartment, Suzanne realized she should have announced that she had an urgent appointment and vamoosed. She thought about asking him to fix the sink while she was gone, but she was...curious. Besides, her apartment was too private a place to let somebody she barely knew walk around by himself, especially someone with a reputation like Greg's.

For one thing, he might find her stash of sexy novels. Jared had made great fun of those. He'd insisted that reading them meant she'd rather get her kicks vicariously than with a living, breathing man. He'd also claimed that no real guy ever acted the way the men did in those books. He was probably right about that, because she hadn't found any so far.

But she should have risked having Greg poke around by himself, because being here with him was a colossal mistake. He smelled too good, too masculine, a combination of lime-scented shaving cream and Old Spice. Nothing fancy for this guy. Much as she didn't want him to, he was turning her on.

She could still leave, of course. She could, but she was already entranced, a deer in the headlights. When he leaned in to turn off the water valve under the sink, his biceps rippled. She'd seen plenty of rippling biceps at the gym both nights she'd dragged herself there with Terri this week, but the guys at the gym were flexing on purpose. A casual, unconscious ripple was so much sexier.

"Can I get you anything?" she asked. "Water, coffee, a soft drink?" *A condom?*

"No, thanks." He sat on the floor and chose a wrench from his toolbox.

The authoritative way he grasped the wrench caused little jolts of excitement to dance in her stomach. Her ideal lover would have sure hands like Greg's, a firm yet gentle touch. She admired his long, tapered fingers and the fine sprinkling of dark hair on the backs of his hands.

He wore a utilitarian watch, the kind you could buy at the drugstore, and no rings. The lack of rings came as no surprise after what Terri had said. He was a Don Juan of the big city, a man who wanted no entanglements.

There would be a certain freedom in making love to someone with that attitude. She wouldn't have to worry about whether he would make a good husband or a good father, or even a good impression on her mother. Most of all she wouldn't have to worry about whether he would leave her, because no commitment would exist in the first place. The sex would be about mutual pleasure and nothing else.

It was a whole new concept for her. Up to now she'd scrutinized every man in her life for warning signs that they would eventually treat her the way her father had treated her mother. No wonder she hadn't ever fully relaxed sexually with a man. So much had been at stake. With Greg, nothing at all would be at stake, and she might finally have the kind of experience she'd read about in her novels.

He glanced up at her. "Maybe you should go ahead and have dinner."

She looked away, afraid that with his experience he might be able to guess her thoughts. "That's okay. I had a late lunch." Maybe he'd misinterpreted her hungry look. Food was the last thing on her mind right now.

"My plan is to dismantle this baby and take it downstairs to see if I have a replacement part. I'm not sure how soon I'll have it back in operation, so I hope that's not a problem."

She couldn't keep avoiding his gaze forever, as if she lacked any self-confidence. So instead she looked at him with the same directness she'd use with a colleague at work. "No problem."

There were questions lurking in those green eyes of his. He probably wondered when she'd start getting personal. He might even be giving her more time to feel comfortable with him by drawing out the repair process.

She'd never feel that comfortable. Suzanne Talbot did not fall into bed with a man she hardly knew. "What's your last name?" The question popped right out of its own accord.

"Stone." Warmth flickered in his gaze. "Thanks for asking."

Heat flooded her face. "I'm not sure why I did. I guess it doesn't really mat—"

"Sure it does. It always does." Without giving her a chance to respond, he leaned back and squirmed under the sink until his head and shoulders were nearly out of sight.

She appreciated his tact in partially disappearing so that she could pull herself together again. Now that she'd asked his last name, he probably thought it was only a matter of time before she invited him to spend the night. He might expect her to use this moment to change into something more revealing.

She wouldn't be doing that, but maybe she'd indulge her curiosity a little more by checking him out when he couldn't see her do it. It wasn't every day that she had a chance to study a certified loverboy up close and personal.

He wore his navy T-shirt tucked into the waistband of his jeans, and no belt. Well, belts were an unnecessary impediment, after all. This looked like a man who appreciated simplicity when it came to clothes that might need to be shed quickly in the heat of passion.

As she watched, he lifted his pelvis and shifted to the left to get a better angle on the pipe. The front of his shirt came untucked and rode up, exposing a neat belly button. An insy.

Saliva pooled in her mouth as she stared at that belly button. Such an intimate part of a person, a belly button. A smattering of dark hair decorated the area around it. He inhaled, causing a slight gap between his flat belly and the waistband of his jeans. A gap just big enough for a woman to slip her hand into, if a woman were so inclined....

She moistened her lips. She wasn't even remotely that daring. Besides, he wouldn't be expecting something like that, and he'd probably sit up suddenly and bean himself on the water pipe.

But she could imagine doing it, and that was enough to get her juices flowing. His jeans were old and the denim looked soft. As he shifted his weight again, the material tightened over his crotch and she gained an excellent idea of exactly what lay behind that button fly.

Greg looked like such a bad boy, and now that Terri had confided in her, Suzanne knew that he was absolutely as bad as all that. Even if she had the courage to come on to him, which she didn't, she wouldn't know what to do with such powerful badness.

But Terri had said that he was understanding and very romantic. In that case, she wouldn't have to know everything. He would know everything, just like the men in the novels she loved.

Yet if she managed to start an affair with Greg, who had become a legend in her apartment building, and she *still* turned out to be an anal-retentive ice queen, what then? She'd probably never date again. She'd channel all her energies into her career, become the best financial analyst in Chicago, make piles of money and live alone in some opulent penthouse with her twenty-nine cats. Rich but pathetic.

If there was the slightest chance she'd blow it with Greg, she'd be far better off blundering along as she'd been doing. The situation reminded her of when she'd had a funky Honda Civic with lots of miles on it. She'd loved that car, but one day it wouldn't go. A boisterous jock from high school, somebody much like Jared, had talked her into letting him give her a jump. He must have done something wrong, because he'd burned out the electrical system.

Getting involved with Greg was a jump start that might blow out her entire electrical system, and she'd have to be towed in, just like that Honda. She was already feeling road-weary after two nights at the gym with Terri. In her present condition she probably wouldn't be able to have sex without pulling a muscle, anyway.

So why, with all those considerations, was she staring at Greg's crotch and getting damp and achy? She liked the shape of his legs, too—long and lean. He wore scuffed running shoes that were some off-brand she didn't recognize, and no socks. His lack of pretense was very appealing, especially after she'd spent so much time with Jared, who was terminally fashion-conscious.

Sex with Greg would mean stripping the act down to its primary motivation—one man, one woman, pure lust. She could guess from Greg's manner of dress and his general attitude that he wouldn't care what brand of mineral water she had in the fridge or whether her sheets had a Calvin Klein label.

She didn't know how she'd fare in the pure-lust department. In her experience, sex had always been more complicated than that. But watching Greg twist his body as he wrestled with the pipe fitting, listening to his grunt of satisfaction when he wrenched the piece free, she certainly felt as if pure lust was a possibility.

As he started to emerge from under the sink, she backed out of the doorway to give him room to maneuver. Here she was, standing conveniently in the bedroom. But even if she chose to start something, she'd have no idea what to say first.

I've heard good things about you, Greg. That sounded way too fake, like bad cocktail-party chatter.

I'm between boyfriends right now, Greg. Oh, that was classy. She'd appear to have a spare ten minutes where she could work him in.

I could use a friend, Greg. Better, but not true. She had friends. What she needed was a lover, a lover who would heal her bruised sexual ego.

He emerged from the bathroom holding the rusted pipe wrapped in a rag he must have taken from his toolbox. "Can I leave my tools here for now?"

"Sure." Now was the time to tell him he didn't have to rush the job. He could put the pipe down and find something else to do with his hands. She should have asked Terri how she'd handled this awkward moment.

"Okay. Thanks." He walked past her and out of the bedroom. He was definitely getting away. "Lock up after I leave, though," he said over his shoulder. "This neighborhood's pretty safe, but there's no need to take chances."

Whatever she needed to say to make him turn around wouldn't come out of her mouth. "Right."

"See you in about ten minutes."

"Okeydokey." *Ten minutes. Time enough to call Terri and get some advice.*

The door closed behind him. She walked over and locked it as he'd suggested. He didn't know that she was very good about locking up. Just ask Jared, who had been caught in the hall without a key.

That doggone Jared—he'd known she was going to the store. She seemed to remember having told him to take a key when he'd left for his run, but maybe she hadn't. She might have assumed he'd take a key to be on the safe side.

Suzanne was always on the safe side. This whole business with Greg didn't feel at all safe. She dialed Terri's number and tapped her foot while waiting for the no-solicitation message to finish. Finally Terri picked up.

"It's Suzanne," she said. "Greg is here fixing my sink."

"Congratulations!"

"It really was leaking, Terri."

"Sure, sure." Terri laughed. "Whatever you say, girl. Enjoy."

"He left to get a replacement part, and he's coming back. Nothing's happened yet, and I was wondering how you got from the handyman job to…more personal stuff."

"Um, well…I said something about how I didn't understand guys at all, I think. He asked me to elaborate, and we…took it from there."

"That was a good line." Suzanne couldn't imagine coming up with a better one, but she could hardly use Terri's.

"He's very sweet," Terri said. "Don't angst over this. Just start talking to the guy."

Anxiety caused her ears to buzz. "You know what? I'm not doing this. I'm not cut out for it."

"That's what you said about the gym, and look at you now."

"Exactly! I'm sore in places I didn't even know I had places. If you're telling me that getting involved with Greg is like signing up for the gym, then I'm definitely not doing it."

Terri laughed again. "You're such a crybaby. Greg won't be anything like the gym. He's—"

The doorbell rang and her chest tightened. "He's back. Bye, Terri."

"Go for it, Suzanne!"

She wasn't going to follow Terri's advice, she decided as she went to answer the door. The sound of Greg ringing the doorbell had nearly made her faint. She didn't have the chutzpah to carry this off, and that was that.

3

GREG HAD THOUGHT SUZANNE might change clothes while he was downstairs, but nope, she wore the same serious businesswoman outfit as before. The velvet bow was still in her hair, too, and the tidy pumps remained on her feet. He couldn't believe she hadn't kicked them off by now.

There was absolutely nothing in her behavior to suggest she wanted to become more friendly with him. He was almost convinced that she had no interest in talking about her personal life. So then why had she asked his last name?

"Luckily I found what I needed," he said, holding up a section of pipe.

"Great." She smiled and stood back so he could come in.

That smile was still full of nerves, he thought. Terri had said something to her—he was sure of it. Apparently Suzanne didn't know quite what to do with the information.

"This shouldn't take long," he said as he walked through the white living room with its touching little Christmas tree and one red pillow. "You'll be back in business in no time."

"That's good." She followed him.

He tried to interpret why she trailed after him when the job didn't require her to be there. He concluded that she was working up to a real conversation.

He gestured toward the devil on his way through her bedroom. "Cute little guy."

"I thought so, too. He was in the kids' department at Marshall Field's, and I couldn't resist him."

So she'd bought the devil for herself. If someone had given it to her, someone like Jared, he wouldn't have placed so much stock in it. But then again, she wouldn't have had to plop it smack-dab in the middle of her bed, either. The devil said something about her, just like the red pillow in the living room.

Guaranteed, he'd found a shy woman who was hiding a delicious naughty streak. His ultimate fantasy. But if she was shy, she might never become bold enough to cross the barrier between them.

That was really for the best, because the longer he hung around Suzanne, the more he realized that he would definitely have trouble maintaining his distance. Suzanne was too close to his ideal woman for comfort. If she indicated the slightest interest he would be setting himself up for a fall.

Once he got to know her better, she'd probably give herself away like all the others had. Sooner or later she'd ask why he hadn't finished his degree. When she learned he had no interest in that, she'd either end the connection or keep bugging him about it. He wasn't about to be harassed.

At least now he knew enough not to repeat the mistake he'd made with Amelia. He was probably an idiot for holding out any hope that he'd find a woman who was smart, ambitious and yet willing to let him live as he chose. Still, the hope wouldn't completely die.

Suzanne lingered in the doorway of the bathroom as he sat down and prepared to wiggle under the sink again. She reminded him of his cat, Matilda, when he'd first found her as a stray two years ago. Matilda had been timid in the beginning, too, but once he'd won her over she'd turned into an awesome cat. He tended to prefer people and animals who were slow to warm up. Although they presented more of a challenge at first, they usually were more steadfast in the end.

Still, he had the impression that he could fix the sink and leave the apartment without making any real contact with this intriguing woman. Once again, he told himself that was a good thing. He was too attracted to her, and that was dangerous.

But what if Suzanne was different? What if she was the one he'd been looking for? On impulse, he broke a long-standing rule. "I haven't seen your boyfriend around lately," he said.

Panic flashed in her blue eyes. "Uh, he—"

"Not that it's any of my business." He ducked under the sink, silently cursing himself. He might imagine he knew what was going on with Suzanne, but he could be dead wrong. All he really knew was that the pipe under her bathroom sink had rusted out.

No, that wasn't true, he thought as he applied plumber's tape to the threads of the new pipe. He'd bet a million dollars that she hadn't been the one who walked out of the relationship. And, as his experience taught him, now she was doubting herself, doubting her ability to attract and keep a man. Restoring the confidence of women in that position had become his stock-in-trade recently, and he knew that he did it well.

In spite of the risk, he wanted to help Suzanne, but he couldn't if she didn't want him to. So far she'd given no indication that she wanted his sympathy and counsel. He inserted the new pipe and tightened it down. At least Suzanne's sink wouldn't leak anymore. As for the rest of her problems, she'd have to decide whether she needed his assistance.

Crawling back out from under the sink, he checked to see if she was still standing in the bathroom doorway. She wasn't. He'd scared her off with that remark about Jared. Served him right for jumping the gun.

He turned on the water valve and tested the pipe coupling for leaks. An interesting word—*coupling*. He hadn't enjoyed any personal coupling in months, not since the mess with Rachel.

About a year ago he'd stumbled onto a cozy pub, a place where he'd felt instantly at home. The weekly darts tournament had soon become a cherished ritual for him.

Rachel was one of the regular participants and they'd flirted with each other for months. But they never should have gone to bed together. Deep down he'd known that, but he let a couple of beers and her sexy red dress cloud his judgment. Rachel was good-hearted, and she had an amazing body, but she had no intellectual curiosity whatsoever.

That's when Greg had learned the hard way that if a women didn't stimulate his mind she wouldn't stimulate the rest of him, at least not after the first flush of discovery had passed. Rachel, as forgiving a woman as he could hope to find, didn't seem to hold it against him. The others had obviously taken their cue from her, so he was still welcomed as part of the group. Because his job could be lonely at times, he needed that connection.

While he put away his tools and closed up the toolbox, he thought about the bind he'd created for himself. The women who attracted him, like Suzanne, weren't likely to want a guy who was content to remain a handyman for the rest of his life. But women like Rachel, who thought his job was perfectly acceptable, weren't brainy enough to satisfy him. He'd boxed himself into a corner, and he had no idea what to do about it.

Walking back through Suzanne's bedroom, he noticed

her suit jacket lying neatly across the end of the four-poster bed. He wondered if that was a subtle signal, and his pulse quickened.

Then he blew out a breath, impatient with himself. Talk about overanalyzing the situation. No doubt she'd decided to cook herself some dinner and didn't want to do it wearing a suit jacket.

Still, he couldn't quite dismiss the picture of Suzanne in the bedroom taking off her suit jacket while he was only a few feet away working on the pipe under her bathroom sink. Thinking of Suzanne unfastening buttons and arching her back slightly as she slipped out of the jacket, he experienced a distinct stirring in his groin.

That impulse had required two beers and a slinky red dress in Rachel's case. Apparently, in Suzanne's case, all he needed was his own fertile imagination and a black suede jacket lying across the end of a bed of roses.

He took another look at the little red devil on her bed. If only Suzanne hadn't asked him his last name, he'd be convinced that there was nothing on her mind besides the sink. But she *had* asked, which made him wonder if the two of them were missing a golden opportunity to get better acquainted.

"See you later, buddy," he said to the devil, although chances were he never would.

He found Suzanne in the kitchen stirring a saucepan full of tomato soup. By eliminating the jacket, she'd raised the seduction value of her outfit about five hundred percent. The cream-colored blouse had long sleeves with covered buttons down the front and at the cuffs. A silky blouse like that draped a woman's breasts like nothing else he knew of. He could make out a hint of lace beneath the material, a kind of subtlety that had always driven him a little crazy.

Moist heat from the stove had steamed up the small window over the sink, which seemed to close them into their own private world. If they were lovers, he'd put down his toolbox and walk up behind her to wrap his arms around her waist. Then he'd cup her breasts. He swallowed, nearly able to feel the warm silk against his palms. Gradually he'd begin unfastening the buttons...

He cleared his throat. "You're all set," he said. "No leaks."

She glanced up, a wary look in her eyes. "Thank you so much."

Had she seemed more relaxed, he might have searched for a reason to stay, but she was as uptight as ever. "I'll be taking off, then." He started to leave.

"Would you..."

He turned back. "What?"

Her cheeks were pinker than the roses decorating her comforter. "Would you like some soup?"

He hesitated, unsure if the offer was made from courtesy because he'd caught her in the act of preparing it, or if she genuinely wanted him to stay.

"It's out of a can," she said. "It's not homemade or anything. And I'm keeping it simple." She nodded toward a cheese board holding a wedge of cheddar and a cheese slicer. Next to that was a basketfull of assorted crackers. "Just crackers and cheese to go with it."

That decided the issue. No way would he turn down her soup and make her think he cared whether it was canned or not, or whether he was picky about having a full meal. "Thanks. That would be great." He looked around for a place to put his toolbox.

"Over there by the pantry is fine."

He set the box down, shoving it out of the way as best he could.

"I've never seen a wooden toolbox like that," she said. "Aren't they usually made out of metal?"

"The newer ones are," he said. "This one belonged to my dad." He couldn't remember any of the tenants commenting on the box, and he was pleased that she had. The toolbox meant a great deal to him, but to most people, it was only a big wooden carrying case. "Can I help with anything?"

She shrugged. "Not much to do but stir."

The kitchen was small and narrow, with the stove and refrigerator on one side, the sink and cabinets on the other. He wanted to wash his hands before he ate, but if he stood at the sink, he'd be crowding her, invading her space. Still, going back into the bathroom to wash his hands seemed sort of ridiculous.

"I'd like to wash up, if you don't mind."

"Sure." She didn't look up from her vigorous stirring of the soup.

The space between was barely big enough for two people. He was careful not to brush against her as he moved in front of the sink. In such proximity he could smell that rose fragrance of hers, and when he leaned over to wash his hands, his hip brushed against her. He imagined he heard a quick intake of breath and wondered if she'd felt the same jolt of awareness he had.

"Sorry," he said. He tilted his pelvis toward the sink.

"Not a problem."

He was a skilled listener, and he heard the tremble in her voice. "They didn't build these kitchens with two people in mind." In reality he thought this was the best kind of kitchen for cooking with your lover. He thought large spaces were highly overrated.

Pulling a paper towel from a rack, he noticed that the screws on the rack were loose. "Your towel rack needs to be tightened up," he said. Yeah, sure. He was looking for an excuse to keep occupying that space.

"Later, maybe. The soup's ready. If you'll take the crackers and cheese into the living room, I'll bring the soup."

He reached over and picked up the cracker basket and the cheese board before going to stand near the kitchen doorway. "We're eating in the living room? On that white sofa?" He had a vision of tomato soup all over it.

"It's stain-proofed." She turned, reached into the cabinet and took out two large stoneware mugs. When she did that, she grimaced, as if raising her arms hurt her.

"Are you okay?"

She turned in surprise. "I'm fine. Why?"

"You looked as if you were in pain just then."

"Oh. I've been going to the gym with Terri, and my muscles aren't pleased about it."

Now he had a new picture to contend with—Suzanne in tight workout clothes. "I don't think you're supposed to get sore working out. Do you stretch?" He wondered why anybody with a body like hers felt the need to go to the gym. No body-sculpting machine would be able to improve on those measurements.

"I stretch." She took the pan from the stove and started pouring the soup into the mugs. "I get in the hot tub. I take herbal baths when I get home."

He'd bet she did. And now he had a mental image of her doing that. Oh, baby.

She gave him a quick smile. "I'm just not in very good shape. It'll get better, or at least Terri says it will."

"A massage might help." This conversation wasn't a good idea. Now he imagined Suzanne stretched out on a massage table naked, while someone, preferably him, oiled her up. He'd sent away for a tantric-massage video months ago because he'd always been curious about the discipline.

He'd discovered that the video showed him exactly how to massage a woman to orgasm. He'd never tried it.

"Massage might be a good idea." Her color was high, almost as if she'd been able to peek into his fevered brain. "I'm sure the gym has some people on staff who could handle that."

"I'm sure." He didn't want her to be massaged by *some people on staff*. He wanted to take care of it, and he wanted to do it now.

She picked up the mugs and glanced at him. "Ready?"

SOUP. SHE'D INVITED HIM to have a bowl of from-a-can soup. How domestic and totally idiotic. When she'd come up with the plan, it had seemed like a great idea for a cold winter night and something she could prepare in a hurry. But Greg was a big guy, and the skimpy meal she'd offered him wouldn't be more than an appetizer for him. *An appetizer for what?*

"Should I move the poinsettia?" he asked.

"Um, sure. And the magazines, if you don't mind. That stuff can go on the end table."

She waited while he cleared the table and set down the cheese and crackers. He used care with her things, she noticed. Jared would have scooped up everything and dumped it in a pile, knocking leaves off the poinsettia in the process.

Concentrating on the task, she managed to place the mugs on the glass coffee table without spilling a single drop. That was a real feat, because she was still quivering inside from the way he'd looked at her back in the kitchen. She couldn't remember ever having a man look at her like that, with such total appreciation. With *carnal* appreciation, to be precise.

She'd always assumed that kind of heated look would

make her feel devalued, like a convenient sex object. But that single look, as if he'd enjoy licking every square inch of her, had done more for her self-esteem in two seconds than she could imagine getting in two years at the blasted gym. No, Greg was *not* like the gym.

But that didn't mean she planned to go to bed with him. Scorching looks were a long way from scorching touches. But you couldn't blame her for wanting to keep Greg around a little bit longer. Maybe she didn't need the full treatment. A few more of those melting looks and she'd be good to go, ready to hit the dating scene, her ego repaired.

It felt great to be sexually desired. Fabulous. She surveyed the coffee table to see what they were missing. "We need napkins. I'll be right back."

She hurried to the kitchen and started to grab a couple of paper napkins from the holder on the counter. Then she changed her mind, opened a drawer and took out the bright red cloth napkins she'd bought because they matched the pillow on her sofa. She'd never found the right time to use them.

When she returned, she found him leafing through one of the magazines he'd moved to the end table. "Looks like you're interested in decorating."

She sat down, keeping a full cushion's distance between them, and handed him a napkin. "I like to fool around."

His glance was warm and knowing as he laid the napkin over his knee. "I can see that."

Her words echoed in her head and she blushed. "With decorating, I mean."

"I knew what you meant." He picked up the mug of soup in those capable hands of his. "And it shows."

She feared that what was showing was her sexual interest in him. She had to be careful that he didn't get the wrong idea and act on some silent signal she was giving off. She grabbed the slicer and carved off a piece of cheese. "It's hard to do much decoration in such a small apartment." She put the cheese on a cracker so that she'd look as if she actually cared about eating.

Cradling the mug, he gazed at her. "Does that mean you want a big house someday?"

A big house, with a big bed, and a man who looked like Greg lying naked in it. "I suppose I do." She'd always expected to have a home, and a husband, and a couple of kids. It was the American way.

In between imagining Greg lying naked on a king-size bed, she found herself wondering about his future plans. Maybe he'd asked the question because he was saving money to get a place of his own. "Do you want a big house eventually?" she asked. Then she took a bite of the cracker and cheese she didn't want but had to pretend to enjoy.

"A house, maybe. Not a really big one, though. I like intimate, cozy spaces."

She choked on a piece of cracker.

"Are you okay?"

Nodding frantically, she coughed and took a gulp of her soup. *Intimate, cozy spaces.* The man had a way with words.

He gazed at her with concern. "You're sure you're okay?"

She cleared her throat and blinked the moisture from her eyes. "I'm sure. Just took a breath when I shouldn't have. So you're hoping to buy a little bungalow, then?"

"Yeah. More like a cottage. I'll probably always work in the city, but I wouldn't mind having a vacation place in Wisconsin. On a lake would be terrific. And it has to have a fireplace."

"Sounds like a nice dream." Nobody would have to talk Greg into snuggling on the sofa on a rainy afternoon or during a weekend trip to a cottage in Wisconsin. Longing shivered through her. She wanted to be cuddled on a sofa. She wanted to be held, stroked, petted. According to Terri, this man knew how to do the job right.

But he was still a virtual stranger, and she didn't go to bed with strangers. "You said that toolbox belonged to your dad," she said. "Was he a handyman, too?"

He looked surprised by the question. "Yeah, he was."

"So you decided to follow in his footsteps?"

"Not at first. Not until after..." He paused and stared down into his soup. Then he glanced up. "Not at first," he said again with a smile. "You know how it is. Kids never want to do exactly what the parents do."

She was positive he'd just made a decision not to tell her something important. Apparently he could talk about his vacation-home plans, but not about his father. He might be willing to take her to bed, but he wasn't willing to tell her his innermost secrets.

Maybe that's how a Casanova had to operate. Confiding secrets bonded people together, and Greg wasn't about that. He was about restoring a woman's sexual confidence and moving on.

Suzanne knew she ought to just accept the rules of the game. Instead she began to wonder why Greg had chosen this loner lifestyle, and if he protected himself because someone in his past had hurt him. "Do you like the work?" she asked.

"Yes. Yes, I do. The pay's not great, but I get a place to stay and I'm pretty much my own boss. I also happen to like these older apartment buildings. I take a lot of satisfaction in keeping the place maintained in top condition."

"I'm sure." And in his spare time, he did the same for the female tenants, both taking and giving satisfaction. Broken light switch, call Greg. Broken heart, call Greg. But who was this man who rode in on a white horse, saved the day and rode away again? She wanted to know what made Greg Stone tick.

"How about you?" Greg said. "Do you like your job?"

He'd smoothly switched the topic of conversation away from him, and she decided to let him get away with it for now. "Yes, I like it." He had nicely shaped ears, she thought. Some men enjoyed having a woman run her tongue around the curve of their ear. Others didn't. She wondered which type Greg was.

"What exactly do you do?" he asked.

His green eyes were mesmerizing. A woman could forget everything if she allowed herself to be caught in that gaze. "I'm a financial analyst with Apollo Mutual Funds," she said.

He nodded. "I thought you did something like that."

"Do I look so much like an economics major, then?" she asked with a tight smile. Jared used to taunt her about that. *You may love playing with stock-market quotes all day, but you don't have to look like you do.* She'd finally figured out he wanted someone who looked as if she modeled lingerie for a living.

"You do look like an economics major," Greg said with an answering smile. "And I think—"

"I know. Don't say it. You think I need to loosen up, dress less conservatively, wear my hair down, stop looking so *financial* all the time." She'd tolerated that speech from Jared, but she didn't have to hear it from the handyman, especially when the handyman kept himself shrouded in mystery.

He took another sip of tomato soup. "I was going to say that I think that looking like a financial analyst is kind of sexy."

"Sexy?" She glanced down at her cream-colored silk

blouse. "Hardly. But then it isn't my goal to make a sexual statement when I go into the office."

"It may not be. That doesn't mean you don't."

She met his gaze and suddenly didn't want to play anymore. "Maybe that sort of flattery works with other women, but I'm not taken in," she said quietly. "I'm well aware of the type of outfit and behavior that men find sexy, and that's not where I shine."

He leaned toward her, his quiet tone matching hers. "Pardon me, Ms. Talbot, but obviously you don't know your *Wall Street Journal* from the *National Enquirer* if you're going to make a statement like that."

Her cheeks grew warm. She'd expected him to retreat, not counterattack. And she was gradually becoming aware that his vocabulary didn't quite fit her image of an uneducated blue-collar worker. "I have some experience in this matter," she said.

"Not enough, apparently."

"And you do?" They'd danced around enough, and now she wanted to rip away the curtain he was hiding behind. "Why don't you tell me what makes you such an authority on the subject of sexual attraction?"

He put down his mug. "Why and how men and women are sexually drawn to each other is one of my favorite topics. I've studied it endlessly."

"Really? In what way?"

His eyes blazed. "I'm going to choose not to answer that, but I can tell you with absolute certainty that when a woman with a great body wears a conservative little suit, many men find it sexy as hell. They're convinced that a temptress is hiding underneath that businesslike exterior, and they consider it a personal challenge to see if they can strew that uptight outfit all around the room, because nine times out of ten they're right."

She drew back, her heart pounding. "But not necessarily. Sometimes they're wrong."

"Sometimes," he said softly.

"They would be wrong about me!"

He studied her for several long seconds. "Would they?"

4

SUZANNE GULPED. This encounter was quickly spinning out of control. One voice, probably Terri's, told her to let that happen for once in her life. But another voice, probably her own scared-rabbit persona, told her to run for cover.

Greg took the decision away from her by breaking eye contact and clearing his throat. "You know what, I really need to be getting back." He stood. "Thanks for the soup and conversation."

"Anyti—I mean, you're welcome." She shouldn't confuse the issue by suggesting that they might get together again. He was too high-octane for her, and once again, she'd play it safe and stay away from a potentially explosive situation.

"I'll get my tools." He walked toward the kitchen.

She gazed after him and knew she was making the right decision. She didn't belong in bed with a man whose jeans fit like that, a man who walked with such fluid grace, a man who probably made love like an angel. A man who wanted intimacy of one kind but shunned any personal revelations of his own.

Besides, he would be disappointed in her, because she wasn't the temptress he hoped to find under her uptight outfit. He might be too polite to let her know, but she would know, and that was a blow she couldn't endure right now.

He returned carrying his toolbox. "If that pipe gives you any more trouble, give me a call."

"I will. Thank you."

"No problem." He glanced around the room. "You really have done a great job with the apartment." Then he left.

Gone. Opportunity had knocked, come inside, fixed her sink, sat beside her on the sofa, fired up her libido and then left. A girl couldn't expect opportunity to hang around forever.

She was glad he was gone, she decided as she picked up the soup mugs and started into the kitchen. Glad, glad, glad. Now she could spend the evening brewing some green tea and balancing her checkbook, listening to some classical music and touching up her manicure.

Boring.

She stood in the middle of the kitchen, a soup mug in each hand, and was struck by the emptiness of the apartment now that Greg was gone. It was a different kind of quiet from the one that had settled in after Jared had left. Jared's departure had meant the absence of his loud voice, a reprieve from rock music at full volume and his need to turn the TV on at the same time, creating a chaos of noise that had driven her to distraction.

If she'd expected to feel that same relief when Greg walked out the door, she'd been wrong. Greg had brought a turbulence with him, no doubt about that, and she hadn't been totally comfortable with him in the apartment. But maybe comfort was overrated. Greg brought the kind of excitement she craved without even knowing it.

She'd thrown away her chance to build on that excitement, to find out a few things about herself. She wouldn't find out much about Greg—he'd made that obvious—and she'd allowed his need for privacy to bother her. Maybe she was using his reticence as an excuse to avoid taking a sexual risk herself.

Greg had suggested she didn't have enough experience to know what did and didn't turn men on. He was right. And there was no better place to get that experience than with him.

The thought made her stomach tumble with anxiety, but unless she allowed Greg to come to her rescue and teach her a few things about herself and her relationship with men, she could very well be facing a future in a penthouse with twenty-nine cats. My God, the man even came highly recommended. If he were a stock he'd be rated triple *A*.

When she thought about it that way, she realized Greg was a heck of a lot less risky than some man she might meet at the gym or at a party. Maybe she didn't know him all that well, would never know him all that well, but Terri wouldn't steer her wrong.

She'd learned to respect Terri's advice. Terri had helped her through several sticky situations at work, and she'd also recommended this apartment building. The gym would be a good thing, too, once Suzanne's muscles adjusted. No doubt about it, Terri usually knew what she was talking about.

Suzanne's hands began to shake as she realized that she was actually contemplating having an affair with the handyman. But asking him to come back to her apartment and using her sink as an excuse was too lame. Been there, done that. No, if she planned to embark on this course, she'd have to be brave for a change. She'd have to initiate the action.

She tried to remember a time she'd done that with a man, and couldn't think of a single instance. Like Sleeping Beauty, she'd waited passively for a prince to come to her. That strategy had netted her men like Jared. If she wanted to do the choosing for a change, to find someone more suited to her personality, she needed practice in making the first move. She could practice on Greg.

She put the mugs down on the counter when she began quivering so much she was afraid she'd drop them. Then she wrapped her arms around her middle and tried to stop shaking long enough to make a decision. *When a woman has a great body*, he'd said. The compliment had been tucked into his outrageous statement about ripping off her clothes, but she hadn't missed it. He wanted her, and that knowledge braced her for taking the big step.

After all, Greg was something that a woman didn't come across very often—guaranteed to please, and certified not to become a bother later on. He was exactly what she needed for this radical change in her behavior. He was a sure thing.

"YOU'RE SPOILED ROTTEN, Matilda." Greg gave the tortoise-shell cat another piece of chicken from the sandwich he'd fixed himself after getting back from Suzanne's apartment. "And we know who's to blame for that."

The same guy would have been to blame if things had gotten out of hand in Suzanne's apartment a little while ago. Her attitude about herself, encouraged no doubt by that idiot Jared, had ticked him off and led him to say more than he should have. A *lot* more than he should have. He'd never been so aggressive with any woman in this apartment complex.

Thank God she'd jumped the way she had when he'd made his speech about the lure of tidy little business suits, or there was no telling what he might have done to prove his point. He'd been so close to grabbing her and kissing the daylights out of her that the slightest invitation on her part would have set him off.

But she hadn't issued an invitation. Instead she'd acted frightened, which had brought him to his senses.

He sighed. All the women he'd counseled in this building had suffered from the same basic problem. They'd hooked up with a guy who'd boosted his own ego at the expense of theirs. By the time the jerk got tired of the game and dumped them, they were convinced they had nothing to offer any man. More than once Greg had wanted to hunt the ex-boyfriends down and beat the tar out of them for the wreckage they'd left behind.

Picturing Suzanne glancing down at herself and announcing that nothing about her was sexy, he'd been ready to strangle Jared. Greg had been blessed with the ability to appreciate *any* woman whether she happened to be thin or plump, plain or attractive. After he'd concentrated a little while on them, they began to take on a glow that made each of them beautiful.

But Suzanne took no effort on his part to shine like a newly minted penny. Her beauty had dazzled him from the beginning, and he couldn't believe that she didn't know how gorgeous she was. Her lack of confidence made him impatient to jump in there and do something about it.

Unfortunately, he was likely to jump in a little too deep this time. Much as he might want to help Suzanne, he had to think about himself—both his job, which he might lose if he wasn't careful, *and* his heart. The job could be replaced, but if he allowed another woman to stomp all over his heart the way Amelia had, he might not recover.

While he cleaned up his supper dishes, Matilda paced the tiny apartment waiting for him to finish. He took a moment to add water to the metal stand holding his Christmas tree, a slightly larger one than Suzanne's. His wasn't decorated yet for the simple reason that he had no decorations. He'd bought the tree on a whim because he loved the smell of evergreen. One of these days he'd pick up some ornaments and lights, but for now he had a nice foresty scent in his little basement apartment.

Come to think of it, he was in the mood for some Christmas music. He picked out three holiday CDs from his collection and loaded them into his stereo before falling into his overstuffed reading chair. With a little *prrt* of pleasure, Matilda jumped to his lap and curled up, purring happily.

He scratched under her chin, using the exact motion she loved. With his free hand, he picked up the book he'd left on the table beside the chair. For the past couple of weeks he'd been on a Dickens kick.

Reading was very nearly his favorite occupation, but because he was a healthy thirty-one-year-old male, making love to a special woman still ranked first. Tonight, no matter how much he tried to concentrate on the trials of *Oliver Twist*, he kept thinking of how great it would be to snuggle with Suzanne.

Finally he gave up, put down the book and leaned back, closing his eyes and stroking Matilda while he thought about Suzanne. The top of her head came to his chin, which made her about five-seven, a height he happened to favor. With his eyes shut he could imagine standing close enough to catch the scent of her rose-scented shampoo. How he'd love to bury his nose in those wild curls of hers before eventually hooking a finger under her chin and tilting her face to his for a kiss—an under-the-mistletoe kiss.

She had a wide, generous mouth, and he liked that in a woman. Or maybe he just liked Suzanne's mouth, especially when she smiled. In his fantasy she would be smiling, waiting eagerly for that first meeting of lips. Her eyes, which could crackle with blue fire, would be soft and dreamy in anticipation of the pleasure to come.

Taking his time, he'd lower his head, watching how her

lips parted as he drew near. Because this was his fantasy, he imagined her wanting this kiss more than any she'd ever had. Her heart would be beating as fast as his, and her hand would steal around his neck, her fingers warm, her touch reminding him that this kiss was only the beginning....

When his doorbell buzzed, Matilda jumped from his lap and loped into the bedroom. He didn't have many visitors, and she wasn't crazy about socializing with those he did have. He wasn't wild about the interruption, himself. His fantasy of kissing Suzanne had come to the good part.

He wondered what emergency had brought a tenant to his door. Nearly everybody used the telephone to summon him upstairs for whatever repair was needed, an arrangement that was fine with him. This basement apartment was his refuge, and besides, he wasn't supposed to have a pet. The fewer people who knew about Matilda, the better.

Whatever had happened upstairs, he hoped it could wait until morning. Having a handyman on the premises meant that, technically, people could call him twenty-four hours a day, but he still considered the hours between eight at night and six in the morning as his, unless someone had a major flood or wires shooting sparks across the room.

He left his cozy chair with a grunt of impatience and crossed to the door. His impatience vanished when he opened it.

"Uh, hi, Greg." Suzanne looked very beautiful and very, very nervous. She'd let down her curly hair, literally, and it shimmered around her shoulders. Instead of her black business suit, she wore a one-piece, long-sleeved jumpsuit, also in black. An oversize zipper ran from her neck to her navel, and he couldn't help imagining what an easy undressing job that would be—instant access.

Maybe the thought had been triggered by the thrust of her nipples against the smooth material. He'd bet his volume of Shakespeare's sonnets that she wasn't wearing a bra under that jumpsuit.

"Is the pipe dripping again?" he asked. Somehow he didn't think it was. Oh, God, what had he started by over-reacting upstairs? And why hadn't she simply called, instead of coming down here?

"No, no, the pipe's fine," she said.

He'd thought so. His heart pounded as he waited for her to say what had brought her to his door. Her appearance down in the basement was a first. None of the other women he'd befriended had ventured down to his place.

There had been an unwritten rule that conversations would take place on their turf, which made the whole exchange seem less deliberate and needy on their part. It was almost as if they hadn't wanted to remind themselves that a man who was essentially a janitor was responsible for making them feel better about themselves.

Suzanne wasn't playing by the rules. He wasn't sure what was up with the provocative outfit, either. If only she'd unburdened herself when he'd given her the chance in the relative safety of her own surroundings, this relationship could have proceeded like all the others. But she hadn't chosen to do that.

Her gaze was filled with apprehension as she took a deep breath and spoke with obvious effort. "I, uh, wondered if I could talk with you about something."

"Okay." Maybe they'd have this conversation with him standing in the doorway of his apartment. That would be different but acceptable. Safe enough.

"Would it be...could I come in?"

Not safe. Not safe at all, to have her standing in the same room where he'd recently been fantasizing a passionate kiss. Yet, to turn her away would be rude, unless he could come up with a reasonable excuse.

He was fresh out of reasonable excuses. "Sure. Come in." He stood back and allowed her to walk past him. She smelled terrific. He had the crazy urge to leave the door cracked open the way his mother used to insist on when he was a teenager and had invited a girl over to study algebra, but he closed the door instead.

Suzanne gazed with obvious surprise at his floor-to-ceiling shelves of books. "Are these all yours?"

Instinctively he threw up a roadblock. "They make good insulation."

She scanned the room, taking in the spot where his book lay turned upside down on the table next to his reading chair. "I like your Christmas music."

"Thanks." He wanted to forestall any more questions and comments about his surroundings. "Can I get you something to drink?" he asked. "A Coke, maybe, or I could make us some coffee."

"Do you have any wine?"

"Uh, no. Sorry." He had beer, but he wasn't about to offer her alcohol of any kind. No telling what the building's owners would make of him plying one of the female tenants with beer.

She twisted her fingers together. "I should have brought a bottle. I didn't think of it until just this minute. Listen, Greg, I'll get right to the point."

"Let me guess. You want to talk about Jared."

"Jared?" She stared at him. "Why would I want to do that?"

None of this was going according to the usual script. It looked as if he'd have to prompt her. "Because it's cathartic, and I'm a good listener." He gestured toward his reading chair because it was the best seating his little apartment had to offer. He'd pull up a kitchen chair. "Please sit down. I'll brew some coffee, and we can—"

"Maybe that's how you've handled the other women," she said, "but I think that's a waste of time." She clenched her hands so tightly in front of her that her knuckles were white.

"It seemed to help them a lot."

"Possibly, but I don't think that simply talking about Jared will help me." Her voice trembled, but she forged on. "So I'd like to skip all the chitchat and get to the main event."

His vocal cords tightened. "I'm a little confused, here. What main event do you mean?"

She swallowed. "I want you to make love to me."

While a choir sang "Silver Bells," he felt as if a pile driver was operating in his chest. "Suzanne, I can't do that." So this was where his idiotic comments had led them. She wanted a demonstration of what he'd been talking about over soup and crackers.

She looked as if he'd slapped her. "What do you mean, you, uh, can't?"

He'd begun to shake as he tried to keep his cool. Inside he was going crazy thinking about the possibility, but the way she'd approached it was all wrong, as if she expected him to leap into a physical relationship with her like a stud for hire.

That was his doing, no doubt. "No," he said as calmly as he could manage. "I'm sorry if I gave you the wrong impression when we were talking before, but I really can't."

"W-what you mean is, you won't."

"All right, then. I won't." He might be an idiot for turning down the chance for a fling with the woman he'd been fantasizing about for months. But the way she'd asked him made it clear that they'd have nothing more than a superficial relationship, and when he'd fantasized about Suzanne, there had been nothing superficial about it.

"I see." As she gazed at him, her lower lip began to tremble.

Oh God, she was going to cry. He knew how shy she was. She'd probably worked herself up to this request, and he'd flung it back in her face. He should have used a little more tact, considering the communication foul-up was all his fault. "Suzanne, listen, what I mean is that I—"

"No, no, I understand." Blinking rapidly, she lifted her chin and backed away from him. Then she cleared her throat. "Obviously I made a mistake coming down here, and now I've embarrassed us both. If you don't mind, I'd like us to pretend this never happened."

Considering that this felt like some sort of wacky dream, that shouldn't be hard for him. Even now, with her standing here, he couldn't believe that she'd just asked him to make love to her. He scrambled for a way to make this turn out okay.

Before he could think of the right thing to say, Matilda strolled out of the bedroom, tail in the air, and pranced right in front of Suzanne before going over to wind herself through his legs.

Suzanne stared at her, wide-eyed. "You have a *cat*?"

"Um, sort of. She—"

"I love cats." Suzanne crouched down, wincing slightly, and held out her hand. "Hello, you pretty thing. What's your name?"

"Matilda," Greg said. He'd noticed the wince and remembered that Suzanne needed a massage. "I try to keep her out of sight."

Suzanne dropped to one knee and continued to hold out her hand. "I know. No pets allowed." Her voice changed to a soft croon. "Come here, Matilda. I used to have a tortoiseshell who looked a lot like you. Come here and let me give you a little scratch."

"She probably won't," Greg said. "She's shy around strangers."

"That's okay," Suzanne said softly. "So am I." She continued to hold her hand out toward the cat.

Greg felt lower than a whale's belly. He'd led Suzanne to the conclusion that all she had to do was say the word and he'd become her lover, a sort of in-house rebound man. She'd worked up her courage to say the word, only to discover he hadn't meant that at all.

At this point he couldn't very well explain that he'd said those things because he'd had some idea that maybe, just maybe, they had a chance at a real relationship, one that might have a future. She didn't want that. She wanted a guy to restore her confidence in every way, including sexually, before she headed back into the dating scene.

He could only imagine what asking him had cost her. And now, after being rejected by him, she would be rejected by his cat. "Matilda was a stray," he said. "So the thing is, she doesn't trust anyone except—"

"Come here, kitty," Suzanne said, ignoring him as she trained all her attention on Matilda. "That's it. You are so beautiful, so very, very beautiful. Come here, sweetheart."

He watched in amazement as Matilda began to advance toward Suzanne like a tightrope walker, testing each step with a front paw before putting her weight down. Nose outstretched, she crept forward until finally she made contact with Suzanne's outstretched fingers.

Suzanne stayed perfectly still and murmured words that Greg couldn't hear, although he strained to catch them. Yet he knew without being able to make them out that they were endearments, tender phrases born of her obvious affection for animals.

Her soft voice, so sweet and musical, pushed gently and persistently, easing through his defenses as surely as a root tendril could find its way through solid rock. She might use that tone with a lover, he thought, his heart twisting with remorse. He could have been that lover, if he were a stronger man, one who could take what she offered and expect nothing more.

A tremor passed over him as he listened to her commune with his cat. He had to assume that her voice had aroused Matilda's curiosity, and that her voice held the cat captive now, as it did him.

He wondered if Matilda had once belonged to a woman, perhaps a woman with a voice like Suzanne's. In the time he'd had the cat, he hadn't invited a woman to his apartment. Because Matilda had run from any guy that had stopped by, he'd assumed she didn't relate well to anybody but him.

But she related to Suzanne, rubbing the edge of her jaw against Suzanne's outstretched hand. Gradually Suzanne began to scratch under the cat's chin, and Matilda lifted her head to allow the caress. Greg stared at Suzanne's graceful fingers moving sensuously over his cat's fur. He'd turned down the chance to know that caress.

"She's purring." There was triumph in Suzanne's announcement. She glanced up at him, her blue eyes soft and eager, much as he'd imagined they would be as he prepared to kiss her for the first time.

His heart thudded as he looked into those eyes. He ached for her with a fierceness that cried out for relief. But on the heels of that relief would come incredible pain when she left him, bound for someone more appropriate than a handyman.

Yet as he sank into a blue warmth as welcoming as a tropical sea, he wondered if the pain might be worth it.

Once he hadn't thought so, but now...now he wasn't so sure.

Then her gaze faltered, as if she'd suddenly remembered the awkwardness between them before Matilda had arrived. "I should go." She stood.

He had no control over a reply that came from deep within his soul. "Stay."

don't care how attractive Greg is, but I'll be damned if I'll beg anybody else."

He swallowed. "Suzanne—"

"Exactly. You're probably the only plant. Because you figure I always come back. Plants. Things would take me home a nervy Dalmint. To be. Clubs. To cover . . . to the . . . "

5

SUZANNE WAS TOTALLY MORTIFIED that Greg would suggest such a thing. His cat had provided a welcome distraction, allowing her to get control over her emotions. She'd hoped that maybe she'd be able to leave his apartment on a positive note. But all the while she'd been petting Matilda and remembering how much she'd loved her own little Whiskers, apparently she'd become the object of Greg's pity.

She must appear pathetic to him, some forlorn creature who had come to his door begging for love, someone so desperate for comfort that when he'd turned her down, she'd forced her friendship on his cat as a consolation prize.

Straightening her spine, she looked into his amazing green eyes. "I would rather clean the basement floor with my tongue than stay in this apartment a minute more. I'm sorry to have disturbed your evening." She started for the door.

"Suzanne, wait."

"Sorry, but I have urgent business upstairs." Her first thought was to call Terri and give that girl a piece of her mind, but that would be admitting that Terri was appealing to Greg, while she was not.

"Please, Suzanne. Let me—"

"Forget it!" At the door she whirled, hurt transforming at last into a satisfying ball of fiery anger in her chest. "I don't care how sorry you feel for me, I'll be damned if I'll be your charity case!"

His jaw dropped. *"Charity case?"*

"Exactly. You're probably feeling guilty because you turned away a needy soul during this season of giving, but here's a news bulletin, Santa Claus. I'll never be that needy."

"This isn't about guilt! It so happens that I—"

"Feel especially generous tonight? Then maybe you should go drop some money in a Salvation Army bucket." She grabbed the doorknob.

"I can't let you leave like this."

"You have no choice."

"Suzanne." His fingers closed over her wrist as she opened the door.

She gasped and turned, her momentum short-circuited by his firm grasp. How dare he touch her. And yet...how magical the connection was.

Her gaze dropped to where he held her in that competent grip that had made short work of the repairs in her apartment. The fantasies she'd spun while he was lying under her sink wrestling with the leaking pipe blended with the fantasies she'd been creating about this man for months.

He held her deliberately, but not tightly. One twist and she'd be free. Yet she couldn't seem to move. Then she looked into his eyes and found them blazing with an energy that took her breath away. "Let me go," she whispered.

"I don't want to let you go." His voice was husky and intimate as he rubbed his thumb slowly over her galloping pulse.

The desire in his eyes had a hypnotic effect on her

senses. If he really didn't want her, he was a master at faking passion. "Because you feel sorry for me?"

His bark of laughter sounded genuinely disbelieving. "Hardly."

"But you said—"

"I know what I said." Holding her gaze, he eased her hand away from the doorknob and nudged the door closed. "I was a fool and I want to take it back."

Her heartbeat drummed so loudly in her ears that she could barely hear "Deck the Halls" pouring from the speakers in his bookshelf. "Because I was nice to your cat?"

He shook his head, smiling gently as he wove his fingers through hers and drew her back into the room.

"Then why?" The dovetailing of their fingers seemed incredibly perfect, but she shouldn't cave in like this. She should leave. "Why change your mind?"

"Because I would be insane to pass up the chance of making love to a woman like you." He guided her slowly past the cat, who was now munching noisily from a bowl of dry food, past his easy chair, past the fragrant, untrimmed evergreen. Beyond was an open door into a darkened room.

She glanced through the door. The interior was shadowed, but light from the living room revealed the bottom of an ivory comforter tucked into the narrow iron rails of an old-fashioned bedstead. She didn't have to see any more to know what lay beyond that door—the point of no return.

A woman like you. She planted her feet as panic set in.

He paused and lifted his eyebrows in a silent question.

"Listen, your instincts were right when you turned down my request," she said. "I'm not what you think. I'm not some sex kitten hiding under her proper business attire. I'm dull and boring, and I have absolutely no imagination when it comes to...to something like this."

His fingers tightened a fraction. "What makes you say that?"

Humiliating experience, she thought, but she wasn't about to describe the times Jared had stomped out in disgust because she hadn't had the courage to try some erotic bedroom game. Jared was the most recent example of a man who'd grown tired of her conservative ways, but she'd had two serious relationships before Jared, and both men had told her in no uncertain terms that she needed to loosen up.

This would be the same story, and she was foolish to think it wouldn't be. "I've given you the wrong impression by coming down here tonight," she said. "You probably think that means I'm really hot stuff, and I'm not at all."

His gaze gentled. "You're afraid you won't please me?"

The tenderness in his voice caressed her frayed nerves and gave her the strength to be honest with him. "Yes."

He didn't come back with some platitude about how she couldn't possibly disappoint him, and for that she was grateful. He seemed to give the matter serious thought as he studied her. "Then before we go through that door, let's take all the pressure off. Neither of us will have any expectations. As far as we're concerned, the next hour or so could turn out to be the most miserable of our lives."

"The next *hour?*"

The corners of his lips twitched in amusement. "You thought we'd be in there longer than that?"

"No, shorter! Much shorter! The gym has partially crippled me, and besides, I barely know you!"

He chuckled. "Then maybe we should start with a quickie and see how that goes. Like when you go to the ice-cream store and get a taste on one of those little pink spoons. Then you can decide if you want one scoop, two scoops or no scoops at all."

She managed a weak smile in response, but inside she was a churning mass of insecurities. "See, that's exactly what I mean. I was never any good at quickies, either. For one thing, it always sounds so athletic, and as we've established, I'm not athletic. I know men like the idea of grabbing some sex on the run, but I can't seem to—" She paused when he shook his head. "What?"

"I don't."

"Don't what?"

"Like the idea of grabbing some sex on the run." His tone was light, but his eyes blazed with steady heat.

"Oh." She gazed into those wonderful eyes and began to wonder if maybe, just maybe, this man would be different. "White Christmas" drifted from the CD player.

"That wasn't what I meant by a quickie," he added.

The look in his eyes held her as surely as his fingers twined through hers, and she was barely aware that she'd begun moving again, moving through that door into his darkened bedroom, coaxed there by an urge stronger than fear.

Her chest tightened and her breath grew shallow. "What did you mean?"

"That you'd have to make do with only one orgasm this time."

Fear brought her to a halt again. "I thought...I thought we were going to have no expectations."

He went completely still. "Are you saying you haven't ever—"

"No, no, I'm not saying that." Her face grew hot and she blessed the dim light so he wouldn't know. Nervousness lodged in her throat. "I have, but I can't always manage...manage that."

Oh God, she'd never talked about such things with a man before. She could fake it, of course, as she'd done a few times before. But in this case it seemed pointless to pretend. Greg wasn't a potential mate she had to impress with her ability to enjoy sex.

"And then there's the matter of me being stiff from the gym," she added.

"Want me to start with a massage?"

"No!" *Too intimate*, her mind screamed, although that sounded silly, considering why she'd come down here tonight.

He stroked her palm with his thumb. "Then we'll take it easy and see how it goes."

That lazy touch and the knowledge that she was inches from his bed was beginning to make her feel aroused already. Maybe she could make love to him all night and climax a dozen times, and yet she knew how easily she could freeze up if a man pushed her too fast. "It's just that I think you're expecting a certain response from me, and I don't want you to be disappointed."

He let out a breath and murmured something she couldn't quite hear over the rich tones of the Christmas carol. It sounded like *damn idiots*, but she couldn't imagine what he meant by that.

"Don't worry about disappointing me," he said. "You couldn't."

Her panic eased a little more. No man had ever said those words to her. Maybe Greg didn't mean what he said, and he'd only spoken to soothe her in this nerve-racking moment before they became lovers. But she soaked up those words all the same.

The semidarkness made believing easier. His face was in shadow, so she couldn't see nuances of expression. Just as well, perhaps.

In the gloom she made out the vague outlines of the double bed. The mattress sat high on the antique iron bedstead decorated with scrollwork, and a small lamp table sat beside the bed. The room was tiny, with barely enough space for the furniture. A door on the far wall opened into what appeared to be an equally tiny bath.

He reached for the table lamp.

"Don't."

He drew back again. "No light?"

"I'd rather you didn't turn it on." She thought of her one-piece outfit with nothing on underneath. "You won't need it." She braced herself for the usual argument—in her experience men were visual creatures who always needed light, and even mirrors if possible. She preferred the mystery of the darkness.

"Okay," he said. "We'll operate by feel."

At the husky note in his voice, excitement zinged through her. More and more she believed that this wasn't a charity move on his part. It might have started out that way, but he was into the moment now.

"But I need you to close the door, so that Matilda doesn't disturb us," he said. "And then it will be very dark in here."

"I don't mind." Her breathing quickened. The darker the better, as far as she was concerned. Maybe then she could pretend she was someone else, someone who wasn't so timid.

Reaching out, she took hold of the handle. As she pushed the door shut, the room changed from twilight to velvet blackness, and the Christmas music became muted background.

"Shut it tight," Greg said. "Matilda knows how to push open a door if it's not completely closed."

Suzanne pushed until she heard the latch click into

place. "What would happen if she came in?" Perhaps he'd had a bad experience with one of his other lovers.

"I'm not sure." His voice drew closer as he released her hand. "She might think we were playing." He cupped her face in both hands. "Of course she would be right."

Suzanne's heart hammered as she felt the warmth of his breath on her face. "Playing?"

"I think playing is a good word for it," he murmured. "Don't you?"

Her breath caught. This was it—she was about to take the biggest sexual risk of her life, but at least she'd be doing it in pitch darkness. From beyond the door came her favorite, "Carol of the Bells." She took it as a sign. "Yes," she murmured. "Teach me to play."

GREG WANTED DESPERATELY to see Suzanne's eyes. This was the moment he'd fantasized, the moment when he turned her face to his before their first kiss. He wondered if her eyes would be the warm blue that he'd imagined, but in the inky darkness he would never be able to tell. He might as well be blind for all the good his vision would do him tonight.

As he'd told her, they'd have to go by feel. And scent. His nostrils flared as he breathed in roses and the delicate musk of feminine arousal. If she needed darkness to give herself to him, then darkness it would be. Maybe another time...no, he couldn't think ahead, not even hours ahead. Loving Suzanne would be all about the present.

Her skin was smooth and warm beneath his fingers. He caressed her like a sculptor smoothing clay—molding her cheekbones with the heels of his hands and tracing the arch of her eyebrows with his thumbs. Although he'd love to see her, not being able to do that sharpened his other senses. He heard her breathing change when he slid his thumbs over her cheeks and nestled them in the corners of her mouth.

He felt the slight tension bracketing her mouth, felt the flutter of her eyelashes. He wanted her to relax, but even the protective covering of darkness hadn't accomplished that. Remembering Matilda's reluctance to let him pet her, he decided to try the same thing that had worked with his cat. That was his goal, come to think of it, to be allowed to pet Suzanne until she purred, to pet her until she arched against his hand and came back for more.

He began to talk to her as he cradled her face, spreading his fingers and massaging slowly. "This lovemaking session comes with narration."

"It does?" Her response was breathy.

He heard fear in her voice, but excitement, too, as if she rode in the lead car climbing to the top of a roller coaster. "That way I won't startle you by doing something you don't expect."

"Oh."

"I'm going to explore your face before I kiss you."

"W-why?"

"Because I like stroking you there, and once I kiss you I'll probably get more...intense...and want to stroke you...in other places."

Her little gasp of reaction pleased him. Gradually the tension under his fingers began to dissolve.

"I love your hair." He pushed his fingers through it, massaging her scalp as he went. "I love the way it slides through my hands and the way it smells." He used the same calm tone that had worked so well with Matilda, although achieving it wasn't easy. His heart beat wildly at the prospect of what was to come, and pressure built in his groin.

Luck must be with him, because he had condoms in the

bedside-table drawer, even though he'd never made love to a woman in this room. He'd put them there one optimistic day, just in case, and now he blessed that impulse. If he'd had to go fumbling through a cabinet in the bathroom, he'd ruin the mood he was trying so desperately to create. One wrong move and she'd startle like a wild animal and bolt. He couldn't let that happen.

"Close your eyes," he murmured. "Close your eyes and let all that bad tension drain away. Leave room for the good tension, the kind that makes you ache to be touched…to be fondled…to be caressed. There. Like that." Once he felt the weight of her head settling into his hands, he knew she was nearly ready for his kiss.

"Wet your lips for me." Holding the back of her head with one hand, he leaned closer, hovering over that wide, sweet mouth. He didn't know how much she wanted this kiss, but he craved it more than air. "I'm going to kiss you, Suzanne." He said her name with deliberation, stroking it with his voice as he cupped her chin and rubbed his thumb over her moist lower lip. "Open for me."

He hesitated a moment more, and she whimpered. The sound set him on fire. She wanted this kiss, too. Closing his eyes, he kept his thumb against her lower lip, holding his place until he could find her mouth. At the last moment he drew his thumb away and settled against the ripe fullness of her parted lips.

His groan hadn't been an intended part of the narration. He hadn't been able to help himself. After months of fantasizing this moment, he was kissing Suzanne, and she was all he'd imagined—warm, velvety, succulent and eager. So very eager.

He'd meant to take the kiss slow, but when she cupped the back of his head and slackened her jaw to allow him greater access, he thrust boldly with his tongue. She answered with another whimper of need.

Fighting the urge to reach for the oversize zipper of her jumpsuit, he buried his fingers in her glorious hair and tried to maintain his sanity. Maybe the total darkness made this kiss seem like the center of the universe to him, or maybe his months of longing had added sensual impact. Whatever the reason, he'd never experienced anything like it.

Joy bubbled within him, seeking an outlet, and he knew how that joy would ultimately be expressed. Eventually his needs would propel him until he was deep within her, seeking a connection that had eluded him until now. He wasn't sure of many things, but this kiss told him with absolute certainty that making love to Suzanne would be the ultimate celebration of life.

Yet that kind of powerful response might scare her. The potential for magnificence would be his secret to be revealed a little at a time, until he thought she might be able to handle the ecstasy that they could create together. He wondered if she had any idea what they had started.

Now, before he lost control, he had to slow the pace. It might have been at this point that other men had failed her. He didn't want to be another in the line of insensitive clods who'd taken a kiss this potent as license to manhandle her. He withdrew from the kiss by small degrees, lightening the pressure gradually, adding little nibbles and flicks of his tongue as he struggled for breath and restraint.

She wanted more. Her hands clutching his head urged him back to her.

Easy, easy, he told himself. She couldn't know he was close to the breaking point, close to the moment when he would forget finesse as blinding lust took hold. Other men might forget themselves in the heat of passion, but he knew from listening to what women told him that heedless lust caused damage, especially the very first time.

Later, when he and Suzanne knew each other better, he might be able to let go and revel in the passion she inspired, but...and there he was again, planning for a future that might never happen. Probably wouldn't ever happen. Now was all he was guaranteed. Right now. And he would make the most of it.

He took a shaky breath and caressed her scalp with the pads of his fingers. "That...was for starters."

She gulped for air. "Some start."

"Yeah." He began to tremble as he contemplated the next step.

"Can we...can we try that again?"

"In a little while." Kissing her on the mouth too closely mimicked his ultimate goal, and he didn't dare do it again right away. "After I kiss you here." He pressed his lips against her chin. "And here." He moved to her throat as he cautiously reached for the zipper there. "I'm going to pull this down."

"Yes." Her voice had a dreamy quality to it.

The zipper made a purring sound as he opened it slightly. "So I can touch you here." He placed a row of kisses along her collarbone. "You taste like honey. Sweet, sweet honey, as if you would melt on my tongue." He breathed in her scent and felt her tremble as he pulled the zipper lower.

With one hand at her nape, he subtly coaxed her to turn toward the bed as he kissed the smooth skin just above the swell of her breasts. "Can you imagine how much I want you?"

"I..." Her sigh sounded like the music of surrender. "No," she murmured. "Tell me."

"I want you so much that I'm shaking." He eased to a sitting position on the bed. "I'm going crazy thinking of cupping your breasts in my hands." The zipper yielded another few precious inches. "I want your nipples thrusting against my palm." He took the zipper down to her waist. "And the fullness of your breast in my mouth."

She moaned.

"In the dark, my touch has to take the place of my sight." He slipped his hands slowly inside the jumpsuit and bracketed her waist.

Just putting his hands on her warm, silky skin nearly drove him out of his mind. Then he guided her in between his outstretched thighs so that her knees could rest against the mattress. If she felt as shaky as he did, she'd need the support.

"I want to touch all of you," he murmured, sliding his hands up higher.

"I want you to." Her voice quivered.

"I'm going to take my time so that I don't miss any part of you." At last he encountered the bottom curve of her breast and allowed his fingers to nestle in the shallow crevice underneath. He paused, letting the privilege of touching her this way register fully in his brain. He felt the vibration of her racing heart as he leaned forward and brushed a kiss over each nipple.

She drew in a sharp breath.

"That's only the beginning." Cupping his hands, he cradled her breasts at last and closed his eyes in gratitude. If tonight was all he would ever have, he'd burn these sensations into his mind. He never wanted to forget the wonder of loving Suzanne.

6

WHEN GREG CUPPED HER BREASTS in his calloused hands, Suzanne nearly swooned with pleasure. In the romantic novels she loved, the heroine was often caressed to ecstasy by the hero's "work-roughened hands." At last she knew what that meant—to be reverently touched by that most masculine of creatures, a man who earned his living by the sweat of his brow.

The texture of his skin against hers underscored the contrast between them. Because he was so decidedly male, she felt more feminine than ever before.

Holding the back of his head, she urged him toward her quivering breasts. "Now," she demanded in a voice made thick by desire.

His low laugh rippled up her spine and weakened her knees. It contained pure male triumph. His fingers flexed, kneading, stroking. "As my lady wishes."

She gasped as his teeth scraped gently over her aching nipple and sensations shot down to her womb. "More." She could hardly believe the command came from her. It sounded like an order from the sex kitten she'd sworn she could never be. But the darkness made her bold. This secret rendezvous made her bolder still.

"Oh, yes," he murmured in a voice rich with anticipation. "Most definitely more."

The smooth, wet slide of his tongue cooled her heated areola and lapped her nipple, flipping back and forth in a deliberate rhythm. An answering throb between her thighs grew more insistent with each flick of his tongue.

His breath whispered against her damp skin. "I crave you," he said. "Crave this." Then he drew her breast slowly into his mouth. The pressure was exquisite—not too much, not too little, exactly enough to drive her stark raving mad with desire.

She clutched his broad shoulders and moaned. Beneath the soft cotton of his T-shirt, his muscles rolled easily as he splayed a hand over her bottom and pulled her closer, taking the caress deeper. She cradled his face, needing to feel the contraction each time his cheeks hollowed, needing to touch the slight bristle of his beard and the firm line of his jaw.

Her thumb found the moist corner of his mouth and she let it rest there, touching the point where his lips moved so sensuously against her breast. In the light, she would never have dared revel in tactile pleasures this way. In the dark, she could focus on his rough breathing and hers, his guttural sounds of satisfaction and the primitive music of his mouth at her breast. Yes, she needed the cover of darkness to discover herself, and he was the first man to willingly give her that.

His tongue curled over her nipple as he sucked, and he bit lightly with his teeth. She hoped he would leave marks so that she would know this had been real. Deep within her nest of moist curls, the throbbing grew beyond bearing.

In the light, she would never have grasped her zipper and pulled it down the last few inches. She was never that forward with a man. But tonight no one would see, no one would ever know except Greg, who would never speak of this night. The zipper rasped softly, unmistakably.

Greg drew in a quick breath. Gradually he took his

mouth from her breast and his unspoken question hung between them.

"I want…" She faltered. Even the darkness might not be enough for her to say what she wanted.

"What do you want, Suzanne?" he asked in a husky voice.

"I'm going crazy. I want you to…"

"Stop?" A smile tinged his question.

"Make me come," she said in a rush, her face nearly as hot as the rest of her. But she was desperate.

"Do you think I can?"

"Yes!" Frustration had taken away her embarrassment. "Just do it!"

"How?"

"I don't care how, okay?" She thought she heard a chuckle and she laid a hand over his mouth. Sure enough, he was grinning. "You're laughing at me."

"No." He caught her hand and kissed her palm. "Never. That was happy laughter." His voice deepened. "There's nothing in the world I'd rather do right now than make you come." He kissed the valley between her breasts, then a spot a little lower, and another lower still.

"Wait." Maybe she wasn't as brave as she thought.

"So you do care how it's done."

Like the others, he expected her to be ready for anything. She hesitated, torn between her needs and her fears.

"Never mind," he murmured. "Come here." Catching her around the waist, he turned her and guided her down to sit between his outstretched thighs.

That was her first contact with the crotch of his jeans and the formidable erection underneath. "*Oh.*"

"Don't let me scare you," he said.

"But you must need—"

"Not yet, not for a while yet."

In her experience, men couldn't stay in that condition for long without getting really cranky. "But—"

"Lean back." He slipped one hand under her breast and stroked her belly with the other. Nuzzling her hair out of the way, he whispered in her ear. "Let me worry about what's going on inside my jeans."

When he put his hands on her like that, as if she were the most precious creature in the world, she didn't have the presence of mind to worry about anything.

His voice was low and intimate as he fondled her breasts. "How are those kinks from your gym workout?"

"Forgotten." This man who repaired rusty pipes and fixed broken hinges also had the hands of a sexual artist. She tried not to think of how he'd become so talented and how many women he'd caressed this way, in between his maintenance chores.

"Good. Ah, Suzanne, you are so soft." He stroked her tummy in ever-enlarging circles, until finally he brushed her curls at the top of her thighs with the edge of his hand. He paused and moved his hand lower, threading his fingers through the moist tendrils. "Sweet Lord in heaven." His breath tickled her ear. "You're naked under this jumpsuit."

"Yes."

"I had no idea."

"I thought—" She caught her breath as he eased two fingers lower yet, stroking once over her trigger point, making her quiver before he continued, parting her gently, entering slowly.

"It was a terrific thought," he said. "And you are so wonderfully wet."

"Mmm." She wanted this so much that she had to tighten her jaw to keep from begging.

His breathing grew harsh and urgent as he probed

deeper. "I guess you really were ready. Do you know..." He swallowed. "Do you know how it makes a man feel when he...when he slides his fingers inside a woman and finds her as wet and hot as you are?"

"N-no."

"He would do anything for her." He brushed his thumb over that sensitive spot, a whisper of a promise. "Anything humanly possible, when she greets him this way. I can feel you tightening around my fingers, wanting this. You are so ready, sweetheart."

"Please." The word slipped past her defenses.

"I will. Oh, I will, Suzanne. But you have to tell me what feels good. This?" He twisted his hand back and forth, rotating his fingers within her heated core.

She gasped. *"Yes."*

"And this?" He began a rhythmic stroke that made her groan with pleasure. "I'll take that as a yes."

His breathing quickened along with hers. "And this?" He rubbed her flash point with his thumb.

She struggled to speak as her body strained with tension clamoring to be released. "Every—everything," she said hoarsely. "Everything feels...good. So good."

Everything is exactly what she got. He seemed to know when to twist, when to stroke and when to rub for the most mind-blowing effect. But he didn't go straight for the goal. Twice when she'd nearly reached the edge, he slowed the pace and eased her back from the brink.

The second time, she gulped for air and called his name.

He nipped her earlobe and his voice was gruff with passion. "I know. But it's better when you put it off a little."

Maybe, but she was going insane. "That's...enough."

"All right. Hang on. Here we go."

Now his strokes had no pause as he drove her up, up, up...and over. *Yes.* Her climax shook her to her toes, bringing with it such abandoned cries that she barely recognized her own voice.

He held her there, his fingers still buried deep, until she sagged against him with a silly smile on her face. "That was...incredible." The word wasn't adequate, but it was all she could think of in her dazed condition.

For her, orgasms had always been surrounded with worry. Would she or wouldn't she, could she or couldn't she? But not this time. From the moment he'd kissed her she'd felt the momentum building, and soon the question of *if* had disappeared, and *when* had became the operative word.

"I'm glad you liked it." He pressed his mouth to the tender spot behind her ear as he withdrew his fingers in a slow, sensuous motion, as if he hated to leave. "So did I."

"You did?"

"Sure. It's exciting to give a beautiful woman a climax she feels like shouting about."

"I did shout, didn't I?" Embarrassment washed over her. "I don't want to get you in trouble. I hope nobody—"

"Nobody can hear. We're in the basement. I superinsulated the ceiling so I wouldn't hear people tromping in and out of the lobby."

And so they won't hear you make love to the tenants, she thought. But she had to be okay with it, because the isolation of this basement apartment and the darkness of this bedroom had been what she'd needed to truly let go. "Thank you for keeping it dark." He'd just given her the best climax of her life, but she was shy about saying so.

"Not a problem. You know what I think we should do now?" He continued to nuzzle her neck.

"What?" She hoped he wasn't about to suggest turning on the light.

"I think that was such a success, we shouldn't push our luck."

"Oh?" Her heart, which had been beating along at a nice, steady, post-orgasm clip, started racing again. He was going to dump her because she wasn't imaginative enough. She couldn't let that happen.

Sliding from the bed, she dropped to her knees beside the mattress.

"Suzanne? What are you doing?"

Taking a deep breath, she ran her hands up his muscled thighs and over his bulging fly to the top button of his jeans. "Pushing my luck."

GREG HAD NEVER TURNED DOWN an offer of oral sex in his life, but he had a strong feeling he'd better turn down this one. God knows he'd love to have her do what she seemed intent on, but there was a frantic manner about her that told him she was charging forward for all the wrong reasons.

She'd opened the top button of his jeans by the time he captured her hands. "Wait a minute, Suzanne." Oh Lord, he was probably crazy for stopping her. He should just let it happen. The idea of her taking his penis into her mouth was almost enough to make him climax. The reality would be unforgettable.

"Wait? Why? Don't you want—"

"More than you can imagine. But I was thinking that—"

"That I'm too much of a prude to do justice to the program?"

He cringed at the self-doubt lacing her question. "You're no prude. A prude wouldn't have come down here wearing a jumpsuit and a smile. But wouldn't it be better if we didn't try to cram every experience into one night? What if we saved something for tomorrow night? And the night after that?"

In the silence that followed his suggestion, he wondered if he'd made the biggest mistake of his life. She was here now, ready and eager to unfasten his jeans. There was no telling what would happen after she left and had second thoughts. Whatever impulse had brought her down here tonight ready to party might disappear by tomorrow morning.

But after he'd given her that first orgasm, he'd become greedy. He was afraid if they made love all night she would decide she'd experienced all he had to offer and she wouldn't come back. If he could get her to stop now, she might be curious enough about what else lay in store that she'd be willing to set up another meeting. With luck he could hold something back from that one, too.

It was a gamble, though, especially because he couldn't see her expression, so he wasn't sure how she'd taken his comments. As the silence stretched between them, he figured he'd gambled and lost.

Finally she cleared her throat. "Greg, if you don't want to see me again, you can just say that. I'm a big girl. I can take it."

He was shocked. He'd never imagined she'd think that, not after the way he'd made love to her. Slipping off the bed to kneel in front of her, he took her face in both hands. "If you're such a big girl, then you should realize that seeing you again, kissing and holding you, making love to you are all I will think about for the next twenty-four hours until you're in my arms again."

"Oh."

"Yeah, *oh.* So the decision rests with you. Do you want everything tonight? Because I could be talked into that in no time. Your choice."

She hesitated. "You want me to come back down here tomorrow night?"

"Yes."

"When?"

"Whenever you can."

"I have to go to the gym with Terri."

"Then after that." He had a sudden inspiration. "Would you like to help me trim my tree tomorrow night?"

"Is that some sort of code for oral sex?"

He laughed. Maybe he shouldn't have, but she was so funny. Apparently she thought men were focused on only one thing. Okay, maybe there was some basis for that belief, even with him, but he had been known to have nonsexual thoughts from time to time.

"No," he said. "I'd really like you to help me trim that naked tree out there." Then he had to laugh at himself. Maybe his mind was running on a single track after all. "Honestly, I'd like to get some decorations on the thing, and it's not so much fun to do by yourself."

"No, it isn't."

Then he remembered that she'd probably decorated hers alone. Well, all the more reason to collaborate on this one. The more he thought about it, the more he liked the idea.

"You wouldn't expect that we'd do the decorating naked, ourselves, would you?"

Now *there* was a thought. But he knew she wasn't ready for that. "No, that wasn't my plan." Maybe someday, if— he brought his imaginings to a screeching halt. One day at a time. One night at a time.

She sighed. "But it might have been your plan, if I could learn to loosen up."

"Listen to me." He brushed her warm cheeks with his thumbs. "You are plenty loose enough for this man. I had a wonderful time tonight, and I can hardly wait for tomorrow night."

"Me, either," she said softly.

"But it's time to say goodbye for now." He took her by the arms and helped her up. "You'd better zip that thing. I'm liable to get something caught."

"Right."

The sound of the zipper told him she was following his directions. "I'm not going to kiss you goodbye," he said, "because I'm a little volatile right now."

"Greg, I feel terrible about that. I think you should let me—"

"Nope. We'll save that for another time," he said gently. "Now go on upstairs." If he'd read her right, she was still feeling a little shy. She'd want him to stay in the bedroom instead of seeing her out. That would work fine, because he could barely walk.

"All right. Good night, Greg."

"Good night, Suzanne. Sweet dreams."

"I expect they will be." Her footsteps moved toward the door. When she opened it, she was silhouetted there for a moment. The Mormon Tabernacle Choir had just launched into the *Hallelujah Chorus*.

Greg thought something that majestic perfectly suited the image of Suzanne standing in the doorway outlined in warm light from the living room. He had to believe she'd come back tomorrow night or he'd never be able to let her go now. What they'd shared hadn't been nearly enough.

Then Matilda, who had probably been keeping watch, walked up to the open door and meowed.

"Hello there, pretty girl," Suzanne said. She stooped down and stroked the cat.

Greg watched Suzanne with hunger in his heart and pain in his groin. She'd asked him if one of the reasons he'd changed his mind about making love to her had been her reaction to his cat. It was. He'd been able to imagine resisting her until she'd crouched down to stroke Matilda and spoken to his cat in such a loving way. Once she'd done that, he'd known he was a goner.

Suzanne stood and glanced his way. "Sweet dreams to you, too."

"I expect they will be," he said, echoing her earlier words on purpose.

"Lock up after me," she said, and there was a note of laughter in her voice. No doubt she remembered he'd told her to do that upstairs. Then she walked away, and in a few seconds his apartment door opened and closed.

Matilda nudged the bedroom door open wider as she came in.

"Hey, Matilda," Greg said.

The cat came over, rubbed against his leg and meowed. Obviously she wanted him to come back into the living room and provide her with a lap, but he had a problem to take care of first.

"I'll be there in a little while," he said to the cat. He winced as he leaned down to pick her up and his jeans pinched. Putting her gently outside the bedroom, he closed the door again, shrouding himself once more in darkness.

The darkness seemed to bring Suzanne closer, and he certainly didn't need light for this. Didn't want light for this.

Gingerly he unfastened his jeans and stretched out on the bed. Reaching toward the bedside-table drawer, he opened it and took out a bottle of almond massage oil. He'd bought it after watching the tantric-massage video, with the idea that he'd try the routine with a woman.

He'd never used it. Now he realized that long before to-night, Suzanne had been the one he'd imagined as the recipient of his new massage techniques. She'd hovered in the back of his mind, the unattainable woman of his dreams.

He hadn't needed the oil to try some of the techniques on Suzanne tonight, but he might work the oil into tomorrow night's session, especially if she'd had a rough night at the gym. He'd need some light—not as much as the bedside lamp would give him, but some. Maybe he'd try one or two votive candles in frosted holders and see if she'd go for that.

Candlelight, Suzanne naked on his bed, almond oil glistening on her breasts...the picture increased the pressure in his groin to overload. Flipping up the small nozzle at the top of the bottle's cap, he poured a little oil into the palm of his hand and slowly rubbed his hands together.

When he finally grasped his aching penis, he groaned with relief. He'd been right to send her away tonight. No man could be a good lover when he'd been celibate for months and desperately craved release.

But how he wished her hands were the ones slick with oil, the ones stroking him to orgasm. How he wished he could sink deep into her at this moment, even if his control only lasted for seconds. What he was doing now was for the best, though. Definitely...for...the...best. Gasping, he climaxed.

Then he lay in the darkness, wanting her still.

7

CHRISTMAS CAROLS SOUNDED so much better in Greg's apartment than they did at the gym, Suzanne decided as she struggled with yet another monster machine that Terri had coaxed her to try. The object of this torture chamber was to try to close your thighs while the machine did its level best to keep them apart.

Suzanne hadn't wanted to climb onto the machine because it looked way too sexual to her, and she didn't want sore thighs tonight, of all nights. Because she wasn't about to say either of those things to Terri, she was sitting on a padded seat, thighs braced against the padded apparatus that was supposed to give her a body like Cameron Diaz.

Terri, of course, was going to town on her thigh machine. "Can't you tell me even a teeny, tiny bit about what happened with him?" she asked as she pressed her thighs together with the strength of an Amazon. There was no need for her to specify who "he" was. Greg had been the single topic of conversation since she and Suzanne had boarded the bus that took them downtown to work this morning.

"I did tell you." With great effort, Suzanne managed to close her thighs one time. Then the machine forced them apart again. The machine had definitely been designed by a man. She'd bet every blessed one of the machines in this hellhole had been designed by a man, an engineer who had minored in history and written a long-term paper on the Spanish Inquisition.

"You told me he fixed your sink and you fed him soup and crackers," Terri said. "You gave me the chain of events, but you certainly didn't tell me what *happened*." She took a swig of water. "The chain of events is the kind of thing a guy usually tells you. A woman knows that's not the important part."

Suzanne gritted her teeth and managed to get her knees together again. "Can't talk," she said. "Gotta concentrate."

"Okay. We'll talk over a mango-strawberry madness."

A half hour later Suzanne dragged herself to a stool at the juice bar. She'd overdone it on the machines tonight, especially the thigh-mangling gizmo, but if she'd skimped on her workout, Terri would have wanted to know why. Suzanne didn't want Terri to be any more curious than she already was.

On the plus side, Suzanne realized, the workout had finally cured the case of nerves that had plagued her all day. She'd been horribly distracted at work, and she was afraid it had been duly noted. Thankfully, nobody suspected the reason except Terri.

But Terri suspected plenty, and she'd been like a dog with a bone ever since this morning. Suzanne didn't intend to tell her any more than she already had, though. Terri might have clued her in about Greg, but that didn't give her a right to hear details. Sharing specifics seemed weird, anyway, considering Terri's previous relationship with Greg. Suzanne really didn't want to think about that.

Terri scooted Suzanne's drink toward her. "At least tell me this. Isn't he the sweetest, most considerate man you've ever known?"

"He's very nice." Suzanne thought of the incredible orgasm Greg had given her and had to agree that he was consideration personified. She hoped Terri would think the flush on her cheeks was due to the workout.

"You're really not going to tell me how it went, are you?"

Suzanne took a sip of her drink before she answered. She was grateful to Terri. More than grateful, actually. She was indebted to Terri for giving her a whole new lease on life. She didn't want to be mean to her, not for a second.

Finally she turned to her friend. "I really appreciate you letting me know about Greg in the first place," she said. "I really do. But it feels uncomfortable to talk about anything that happened between Greg and me, because you and Greg...well, you were involved, and—"

"I need to tell you about that."

"Oh, please don't." Suzanne was so afraid that Terri would describe her love affair with Greg in detail. That had been another reason for Suzanne to keep quiet, because if she confided in Terri, Terri might feel compelled to confide in her. Greg's intimate activities with another woman, especially a friend like Terri, would constitute *way* too much information.

"This is important," Terri said.

"You know what? Let's just respect each other's privacy and let it go at that, shall we?"

"I didn't sleep with him."

Suzanne nearly tipped over her drink. "You didn't?" Oh, joy, Terri hadn't gone to bed with Greg! But hot on the heels of that happy thought came a million questions. "Isn't that what you were talking about when you said he was such a great rebound man? How could he be your rebound man if you didn't sleep with him?"

Terri gazed at her. "If you breathe a word of this to anyone, I will personally sneak into your apartment and pour red wine all over that white sofa of yours."

Suzanne opened her mouth to give her solemn promise.

"Never mind," Terri said before Suzanne could say anything. "You keep secrets better than me. I swore to myself that I was never going to tell anybody, but here I am blabbing it, after all. But I can't let you go on believing we were lovers, especially since it bothers you."

"It doesn't *bother* me, exactly."

"Yes, it does."

"Okay, it does. The thing is, I don't know any of the other women." And now she was morbidly curious about them. "But I do know you, and that's the difference."

"I don't blame you a bit," Terri said. "I should have told you the truth in the first place."

She couldn't help wondering if Terri was protecting her. "You don't have to say you didn't sleep with him to spare my feelings. I just didn't want to hear the details."

"We kissed. That's it. And the kiss was totally my idea, I'm sure."

Suzanne was skeptical. After all, Terri was a beautiful woman, one she could easily imagine Greg wanting to kiss. She'd rather *not* imagine it, though.

"Hey, I'm not thrilled to admit this," Terri said. "Trust me, I wouldn't, except that I can tell you're freaked out about the idea of me going to bed with him and I hate to have you go through mental anguish for nothing."

Suzanne was beginning to realize that she'd underestimated Terri's commitment to this friendship. Maybe coming to the gym wasn't all about building a better body. Maybe they'd build a deeper relationship in the process. "Thank you." She took a deep breath. "I have to admit I do feel better."

"Good."

"But I'm not sure why you wanted me to think that you had."

Terri shrugged. "Stupid pride. I didn't want to be the exception, the only one he didn't sleep with, so when it didn't happen between us, I decided to keep that to myself. As far as the other women know, I did."

"So you've met the others, then?"

"Just two, but somehow word travels in this little sisterhood."

"Surely he doesn't say anything?" The thought of others knowing about her adventures with Greg gave her cold chills.

"God, no. He's the soul of discretion. It's more of a grapevine thing among the women themselves. So if you keep your mouth completely shut, no one will know one way or the other." Terri's grin was self-deprecating. "My ego pushed me to imply I'd slept with him." She stared into the contents of her drink. "The funny thing is, he made me feel better about myself *without* taking me to bed than any man who's made passionate love to me."

Suzanne nodded. "He can do a lot with one look."

"Don't you know it. He can look at you with such appreciation that you see yourself in a whole new way."

"Yes."

Terri reached over and squeezed her hand. "I won't pester you for any more info. From the expression on your face, I'm going to guess that he decided to get a little more...friendly with you than he did with me. That's okay. Whatever works."

Suzanne wasn't sure how to react so that she wouldn't give away more than she already had. "I...you see, it's only—"

"I understand, sweetie. He's wonderful, but you and I both know it's a short-term thing, no matter how great he makes you feel. He's not interested in commitment and you don't want to get heavily involved with a guy who's basically the janitor in your apartment building."

Suzanne blinked. "What does that have to do with anything?"

"Think about it. You're a highly educated professional. I doubt if he has more than a high-school diploma. You'd be out of balance with a guy like that. You can't spend your lives in bed together, so what would you talk about after the sex?"

Suzanne thought about the floor-to-ceiling bookshelves in Greg's apartment. He'd pretended the books were simply insulation, but she'd noticed *Oliver Twist* lying beside his chair, as if he'd just put it down when she'd rung his doorbell. She also thought about some of the vocabulary he'd tossed into their conversation.

"See what I mean?" Terri drank the last of her smoothie. "Greg understands women like no guy I've ever known, but that would only take you so far in a long-term relationship. He understands that, too, which is why he doesn't try to make these instances into something more. He knows it would be very awkward if he tried. That's what makes him so special."

"I guess you're right," Suzanne said. She knew without asking that Terri had never been down to Greg's apartment. If she had, she wouldn't be saying these snobbish things.

Maybe none of the women had ever been down to Greg's apartment. Maybe she was the only bold-as-brass female who had rung his doorbell dressed in a jumpsuit and a smile. Her face heated as she wondered what he must think of her forward behavior and if he realized how out-of-character it was for her. He had to. She'd acted so uptight otherwise, with her request that they keep the lights off.

"I'll only ask one more thing," Terri said. "Are you seeing him again?"

"Um, yes." Her exhaustion from the workout began to fade and butterflies invaded her stomach again. She still hadn't decided what to wear or how to act when she returned to Greg's apartment tonight. How did a girl dress for a night of tree-trimming and seduction?

"Good. You've been so down ever since the breakup with Jared, so I'll bet you can really use the ego boost. Greg is so good for that."

"But what about his ego?" Suzanne asked. "I mean, aren't we all sort of using him?"

Terri laughed. "I think his ego is in fine shape. I'm sure he takes great satisfaction in putting us back together after a failed romance. Come on, what guy wouldn't like to be in his shoes? From what I understand, there are many men who settle for monogamy as a last resort. Quite a few of them would love to have a harem if they thought they could get away with it. In a sense, Greg's created one in our apartment building."

"I suppose." Suzanne didn't want to think about that. Right now she wanted to believe she was special, not one in a line of needy females. Greg had made her feel that way, as if being with her was like a gift to him. Despite what Terri said, Suzanne wondered if Greg was happy with his role in the apartment building. She couldn't shake off the feeling that he was one lonely man.

GREG USUALLY PUT OFF his shopping until Christmas Eve. But while he was out in search of ornaments and lights for his tree, it had started to snow, and watching kids climbing on Santa's lap in Marshall Field's he was filled with the spirit of the season. Consequently he'd come home laden with presents for his mother, his sister and two brothers.

Christmas had gradually become fun again for his family, especially now that his sister and brothers were old enough to contribute financially to the household instead of draining money from it. He could hardly believe that his youngest brother was a sophomore in high school and his little sister was dating a guy who she might very well marry.

He looked forward to spending Christmas Day with everybody in Joliet. Although his father was still missed, would always be missed, the grief had become less with each passing year. They could tell stories about him now without anybody bursting into tears.

While Greg had shopped for ornaments, lights and tinsel, Suzanne had been on his mind constantly, especially when he'd picked out the scented votives he hoped to use to light his bedroom tonight. He was more than a little worried that she wouldn't show at all.

After a quick dinner that he barely tasted, he stashed his family's presents in the bedroom closet. Then he set out the tree decorations in the living room and arranged his two votive candleholders, along with a small box of matches and the bottle of massage oil, on his bedside table.

He'd thought about buying wine but had dismissed the idea. Wine might relax Suzanne, but it dulled the senses. He didn't want her senses dulled, not even slightly. Earlier in the day he'd put fresh sheets on the bed and cleaned the apartment from top to bottom, much to Matilda's disgust.

Finally he had nothing more to do except put on the new Christmas CDs he'd bought, all of which had a definitely romantic tone to them, and wait for Suzanne to arrive. Or not. The possibility that she wouldn't arrive made him so restless that he couldn't settle down and read to pass the time, so he paced, which drove Matilda nuts.

After following him around the apartment a few times,

she apparently became tired of that nonsense and curled up in his reading chair by herself. Every once in a while she'd raise her head to look at him as if she thought he'd lost his mind.

Which he had. He couldn't remember the last time he'd been so nervous because of a woman. Well, yes, he could, and there was the rub. The last time a woman had tied him up in knots like this was when he'd been dating Amelia.

Suzanne was nothing like Amelia, so obviously he wasn't looking to replace his long lost love. Amelia had been a redhead, a spoiled redhead he now realized. She'd been going to school on daddy's money, and she hadn't been in pursuit of a career so much as she had been trolling for a college boy to marry.

Mainly he'd been attracted to her looks, and because he'd been only twenty he excused himself for such shallowness. Suzanne's looks figured into this attraction, too, but he already liked *who* she was a lot more than he'd ever liked Amelia.

For one thing, Suzanne had an independent streak that he admired. But underneath that determined independence was a vulnerability that awakened his protective instincts. All of the women he'd counseled had been vulnerable, but Suzanne seemed even more easily wounded by the wrong kind of guy. He guessed that she'd had nothing *but* the wrong kind of guy.

Maybe tonight, while they trimmed the tree, he'd find out something about her family. He loved searching for clues about someone by asking about their background, but in this case he was more than casually interested. Suzanne viewed the relationship as temporary, and it might turn out to be. Intellectually he knew that he didn't have much of a chance with her. But his gut was telling him something entirely different.

Yet if she didn't come down tonight...he glanced at the old Regulator clock on his living-room wall for the thousandth time. When the doorbell buzzed, he jumped almost as high as Matilda, who ran into the bedroom as usual.

"It's okay, Matilda," Greg heard himself say as he headed for the door. "It's only Suzanne." *Only Suzanne.* Like Michael Jordan was *only* a basketball player.

All day he'd wondered what she'd wear tonight. Something easy to get out of, like the zippered jumpsuit? That would be very nice. Very nice indeed. Heart pounding, he opened the door.

She looked gorgeous, as always, but so dressed, like a person going to a tree-trimming party where there would be dozens of guests. She wore two red sweaters, a coordinated thing that he'd heard his sister call a twinset. Her skirt was black and short, and her suede boots were zipped up tight around her calves. She wore patterned black stockings. He suspected they were panty hose. He had a long-standing dislike of panty hose. When it came to seducing a woman, there was simply no dealing with them.

He'd guess from the way the sweater combo draped her breasts that she'd worn a bra tonight, too. No easy access this time, although at least she'd left her hair down. Ah, well. Maybe she intended to make this a challenge. Or maybe, and this was a depressing thought, she intended to help him with the tree and then leave. He should have bought the wine, after all.

She held a small red gift bag with green tissue paper sprouting out of the top. Although he'd considered kissing her when she first arrived, the protective way she held the gift bag with both hands in front of her didn't seem to invite that. He'd told himself to read her signals and work from there, to be sure he didn't overpower the situation because he wanted her so much.

"Hi," he said as casually as he could manage as he stepped back so she could come in. "How was the gym?"

"Don't ask. I may be crippled for life." Her tone was light, but her manner was shy as she came into the room.

The scent of roses came in with her, and one breath of that and he no longer cared how many clothes she had on, or whether she was clutching that bag like a talisman to ward off sex maniacs like him. He was ready to take the bag away from her and proceed to remove every stitch she had on. He'd heard somewhere that women liked to be ravished. It sounded like a plan.

But he'd suggested the tree trimming, and if he could be rational for a moment, he really did want to have a chance to talk to her—just talk, so he could find out more about her. At least he thought he wanted to talk. That sweater material looked very, very soft, though, like cashmere. He wanted to touch it. He wanted to take those sweaters off. Now.

After he closed the door she handed him the bag. "I ran out on my lunch hour and bought an ornament for your tree."

He was stunned. "Thank you." He took the bag and opened it. She'd bought him a Christmas ornament. He wondered if she realized that by doing that, she'd guaranteed herself a place in his life forever. His family always kept special ornaments from year to year and remembered where each one had come from.

Unwrapping the tissue paper around the ornament, he discovered that it was a miniature book, a tiny version of *The Night Before Christmas* with a ribbon attached so it could be hung from a branch.

"I wanted an ornament that would fit in with all your books," she said. "A symbol of all that reading."

He glanced into her eyes and saw something he wasn't

used to finding in a woman's gaze—intellectual interest. "This is great," he said with a smile. "And very flattering. But how do you know I don't keep all these books around just to impress women so I can convince them to sleep with me?"

She regarded him steadily. "Do you?"

"No."

"I didn't think so." Her color was high, and there was a slight tremble in her voice.

She was going to stay past the tree trimming. He knew it without a shadow of a doubt, and his heart beat faster. To hell with the tree. He could trim the damn thing tomorrow. There was no good reason to trim a Christmas tree when they could be—

She broke away from his gaze and glanced over at the tree. "Looks like you're all set, here." She crossed to the pile of ornament boxes, garlands, tinsel and lights just as Matilda came out of the bedroom. "Oh, there you are, pretty girl! I was wondering when you'd come out."

Crouching down, she stroked Matilda from stem to stern, exactly the way Matilda liked to be petted. The cat arched her back, obviously enjoying the caress. And all Greg could think about was the way Suzanne had started working on the top button of his jeans the night before and how willing she'd been to stroke him the way she was now stroking the cat.

"There's something for Matilda in the bag, too," Suzanne said.

Greg had thought the tissue paper in the bottom was for extra padding, but he dug around and pulled out a red-and-green catnip mouse. "Hey, she'll love this. But you should give it to her, so she knows it's from you."

Suzanne glanced up with a smile. "Okay." She held out her hand.

He walked over and gave her the mouse, lightly brushing her hand in the process. Oh, man. Contact. The effect was like touching a live wire, and yet he was determined to take it easy. Obviously she wanted to trim the tree. They'd trim the tree.

He watched as she dangled the mouse by the tail, teasing and playing with Matilda until she finally relented and gave the cat her toy. Matilda immediately rolled on the floor in ecstasy, the mouse between her paws.

Greg understood Matilda's reaction. He had the urge to react the same way.

Suzanne's playfulness with the cat was definitely giving him ideas. Playfulness was a good sign. A very good sign. He could build all kinds of fantasies on playfulness.

She stood. "There's one last thing in the bag."

"Yeah?" Grinning, he fished in the bag once more. "This is turning out to be like those miniature cars in the circus with all the clowns piling out." His fingers closed around something plastic, and he pulled it out. Fake mistletoe.

His gaze found hers, and his pulse quickened.

Her cheeks were flushed, her eyes bright. "I didn't want to take a chance on the real kind, because of Matilda."

His chest tightened in anticipation. "I've wanted to kiss you ever since I opened the door."

Her voice was husky. "Well, now you have an excuse."

8

SUZANNE HAD DECIDED to take more initiative for what happened in this love affair. With Greg she was going to be the kind of woman who did the unexpected, the kind of woman she'd never been before. So she'd put mistletoe in the bottom of the bag. Judging from the way he dropped the bag and pulled her into his arms, it had been a welcome idea.

He held her close with one arm tight around her waist, while he dangled the mistletoe over her head with his free hand. "Do you realize we've only had one kiss?"

She slid her arms around his neck, her heart thumping so loud she could barely hear him or the mellow Christmas music on the CD player. But she was good at reading lips, and she loved reading his. "And it was *quite* a kiss," she said in that breathy voice that came upon her at moments like this with Greg.

"It was in the dark." He traced the sprig of mistletoe over her eyebrows and feathered kisses there before leaning back to study her, as if trying to decide where to place the mistletoe next.

She had a sudden image of all the private places he could dangle that mistletoe. She'd never had thoughts like that with a man. "I...I needed the darkness last night."

"I know," he said gently. "Darkness can be sexy, too." He trailed the mistletoe over her cheekbones and followed it with more light kisses.

"I might still need it...later."

"Whatever you want, you get." He looked into her eyes as he stroked the mistletoe along the line of her jaw.

She trembled, thinking of what would happen before the night was over, and she wondered how bold she might become in the heat of his loving. For now, she savored seeing herself reflected in his green eyes. He truly could make a woman feel beautiful with such intensity.

Then his eyes fluttered closed as he leaned down and placed kisses all along her jaw. Every time his velvet lips brushed her skin, her heart beat a little faster and the throbbing between her thighs became more insistent.

When he opened his eyes again, he seemed to be studying her the way an artist would judge a work in progress. "I'm glad you don't need darkness right now," he said, his voice roughened by emotion. "This way I can watch your eyes. The more you become aroused, the softer they are, like blue velvet. I love knowing that you want me."

"As if there could be any doubt." She was surprised that a man who attracted women so easily, a man who had a reputation for being an amazing lover, would need that kind of validation.

At last he brushed the mistletoe over her mouth. "In the beginning, there's always doubt." Then he closed those incredible eyes, and his lips found hers.

No doubt. None whatsoever. His mouth fit hers perfectly. Everything that had ever been wrong with kissing other men was right with Greg. He knew how to breathe, how to tease, how to coax her to deepen the kiss until she was quivering and ready for more, so much more.

Warmth flooded her and she snuggled close, seeking his heat. He moaned softly against her mouth, shifted the angle and carried the pleasure to greater heights. He was a virtuoso, and she would love to spend the rest of her life kissing him. *The rest of her life.* Unnerved by that thought, she drew back, gulping for air.

"Suzanne?" He struggled for breath. "Did I...did I do something...wrong?"

"No," she said in a throaty murmur. She searched his face and wondered how many women had been kissed thoroughly by Greg and had yearned for those kisses to last forever. "You're doing...everything right."

"Then why did you pull away?"

She could hardly tell him that his passionate kiss had fooled her into thinking that she actually meant something to him. That wasn't the way the game was played with a man like Greg. She'd been about to put too much of her heart on the line with that kiss, and she needed time to regroup.

Giving him a quick smile, she moved reluctantly out of his arms. "My fault. I shouldn't have told you about the mistletoe until after we'd trimmed the tree. You said you wanted to do that first—I mean, before we—" She wasn't brave enough to say it, and her face grew even warmer than the rest of her.

"Before we made love." His voice was tight with sexual tension. "I did say that. But I'm willing to change the order of things."

She could tell by the bulge in his jeans that he was more than ready to change the order of things. She wasn't. Decorating the tree would give her time to remember why she was here. She'd chosen to become Greg's lover because she needed to increase her self-confidence, especially in the bedroom. She wasn't here to fall in love with him, no matter how beautifully he kissed.

"Let's decorate your tree," she said, "and save the mistletoe for...afterward."

"All right." His hand trembled slightly as he tucked the

sprig in the pocket of his burgundy T-shirt. Then he cleared his throat. "Can I get you anything? Something to drink?"

"I'm fine, thanks. But go ahead, if you want something." The way she was still shaking from his kiss, she might choke or spill if she had a glass of anything liquid in her hands. She made a mental note to use extreme care with his ornaments to make sure she didn't break any.

"No, I'm okay." Some of the tightness was gone from his voice, and he sent her a gentle smile. "I just wanted to make sure I wasn't being a bad host."

His comment made her wonder again if she'd broken some unwritten rule by coming to his apartment. "I didn't really mean for you to treat me like a guest or put you to any trouble."

He chuckled. "Believe me, you're no trouble. Any man would count himself lucky to have a visitor like you."

She drank up his compliment like a woman dying of thirst. She had trouble remembering that he probably said such things to all the women he'd become involved with in the apartment complex. "Even so, maybe I should have invited you to come up to my place tonight, instead."

His gaze sharpened. "Why? Would you be more comfortable there?"

"No, I really like it here," she answered honestly. His apartment felt like a safe harbor from which to set out on a journey of the sexual unknown. She glanced over at Matilda, who had abandoned her catnip toy to go curl up in the overstuffed chair for a nap. "Besides, I enjoy your cat."

SHE LIKED HIS CAT. That was something, he supposed. He'd give anything to know why she'd pulled away from his kiss. She'd been into it, and then something had scared her.

He hoped it wasn't the fact that she was responding so

enthusiastically to the kiss of a guy who worked as a janitor. So far he hadn't detected any snobbery in her, but it could be lurking there, ready to come out about the time he let down his guard and allowed himself to start believing she was different from the rest.

"Where I come from, we start with the lights." He leaned down and picked up one of the boxes he'd bought today.

"Is there any other way? But you have to test them first."

"Absolutely." He pulled out the slotted cardboard holder and crouched down behind his reading chair, where the nearest outlet was tucked behind his bookshelves. He had to move a couple of volumes of an encyclopedia to get to it. "If you'll open the other box, I'll test them both at the same time."

"Sure."

Unwinding the plug, he stuck it in the outlet and a hundred tiny lights winked on. "This one's good to go." He unplugged it and turned to exchange it for the second strand. He caught her staring at him with the saddest expression. She wasn't quite in tears, but close to it.

Instantly she brightened and handed him the untested lights. "Don't you love the multicolored kind best? Terri thought I should get all white for mine, to go with my decor, but—"

"Suzanne, what's the matter?" He was an idiot. She'd probably decorated a tree with Jared last year, and doing it with him was stirring up memories she'd rather forget. Way to go, bozo.

"The matter? Why do you think something's the matter?"

"The way you looked just now." He stood. "We don't have to do this. I should have realized you spent last Christmas with Jared, so trimming this tree with me is probably the last thing in the world you want to do. Let's forget it, okay?"

She gazed up at him, and in that moment she looked about twelve years old. "It's not about Jared. I guess you could technically say we decorated a tree together, but I mostly did it and he mostly watched football and gave directions. It wasn't what you'd call a tender memory."

He was beginning to wonder if Jared had created any tender memories with Suzanne, a woman who would probably thrive on a steady diet of them. So would most women, but Suzanne seemed to need them more than air. "Then what made you so sad?" he asked.

She looked down at the package of lights she held and ran a finger along the edge of the cardboard holder. "Something about seeing you crouched there, with your face in the glow of those Christmas lights, reminded me of my dad testing the lights when I was a kid."

His heart squeezed as he recognized the sound of loss in her voice. He hoped nothing terrible had happened to her father, but this was exactly why he'd wanted to decorate the tree with her, he reminded himself. He wanted to learn more about her so that he could figure out if his instincts could be trusted or if they were merely the product of his lust.

"I'm sorry," he said.

She glanced up at him. "There's no need to be. I had no idea I'd have that reaction. My parents have been divorced for years, so I don't know why it hit me now."

At least her father was alive, he thought. But a divorce brought its own kind of grief. "There's not always a good explanation for emotions," he said. "They just are."

He could come up with a possible reason why she might be feeling the effects of that long-ago breakup of her family, but he wasn't about to offer his explanation. Their relationship was too new for him to start speculating about her state of mind.

But he thought she might be starting to yearn for a family of her own. That was pure conjecture on his part, but somehow he believed it. If he was right, this season was sure to make that yearning greater. He should know. Watching the little kids on Santa's lap today had made him long for a child of his own—a sturdy toddler he'd carry on his shoulders when they went to visit Santa on a snowy afternoon.

She took a deep breath. "Well, we're not making much progress on this tree, are we?"

"Are we on a time clock?"

"I guess not."

He held her gaze, revealing his desires. He wanted to make sure she kept his intentions in mind. That would build the excitement between them and make the ultimate joining that much sweeter. "I don't know about you, but I have all night," he said.

God, how he loved the sound of that. All night with Suzanne. Of course, he wanted to spend a good part of it in bed, but he couldn't have a bad time no matter what they did, so long as she was with him.

Her cheeks turned pink. "I suppose...I suppose I should get some sleep sometime tonight. Tomorrow's a workday, and—"

He grinned at her. Her determined practical streak was adorable, and so doomed. "Are you trying to tell me to get a move on? I've already told you we can skip the tree trimming."

Her blush deepened. "No, no, let's trim the tree." She thrust the lights at him. "You test these, and I'll start putting that strand on."

"All right," he said softly, continuing to smile at her.

"You're the boss." He thought she might have a slight case of the jitters, but another kiss would fix that and make her forget all about the time.

Still, he wouldn't insist they go straight to the bedroom, even if he thought he could convince her to do it. He wanted to talk to her, and once they entered the bedroom, they wouldn't be talking.

Turning, he crouched beside the outlet and plugged in the second set of lights. "Do you see much of your dad?" he asked.

"Not much. He remarried, had two more kids. So—"

When she paused and let the silence lengthen, he prompted her. "So?" He unplugged the lights and glanced over his shoulder.

Although she'd nestled a few of the lights in the top branches, she'd stopped working and was looking at him. "Fair is fair," she said. "If I tell you about my father, you have to promise to tell me about yours."

Now *there* was a shocker. She was curious about his family. If all she wanted was a brief affair, he couldn't imagine why she'd want to know something like that. He filed the information away.

"Okay," he said slowly. "I promise." He stood. "What were you going to say about your dad?"

She shrugged and went back to stringing the lights on the tree. "Just that I've always felt sort of like an outsider at his house."

He couldn't believe anyone wouldn't welcome this beautiful woman into their home. As she lifted her arms to arrange the lights, the soft material of her sweater hugged her breasts and he couldn't take his eyes off her.

"And besides, my mom never really recovered from the divorce," she continued. "She hasn't remarried, and I'm sure whenever I spend time at my dad's, it's hard for her."

"Sounds like a tough situation." And he wanted to help soothe the hurt. He didn't think making love to her would be enough for that, though. She'd been effectively cut off from her father, both by his new family and her mother's subtle pressure. That might explain why she'd let a dope like Jared dominate her, if she craved a solid male presence in her life.

"Oh, it could be worse." She sounded unwilling to pity herself. "And now it's your turn." She glanced over her shoulder at him. "Last night in my apartment, when I asked you about following in your father's footsteps, you didn't finish telling me about that."

He gave her the short version of the story. "He died."

"Oh, Greg." She lowered her arms and turned toward him. "Was it sudden?"

"Yeah." The phone call from his mother had ended his innocence. He'd never thought about death before then. "Heart attack. He was only forty-five."

"That's terrible." Sympathy shone in her eyes. "That certainly puts my situation in perspective."

"Neither one of them is any damn good," he said easily. In the years since that day, he'd worked through his grief and anger, but there was still a sore spot in his heart, one that might never heal completely.

"No, I guess they're not," she agreed.

As he gazed at her, he longed to hold her so much he could taste it. He could hardly wait to offer her both pleasure and comfort. And, to be honest with himself, he wanted comfort from her, as well. Time to get the tree trimmed so they could move on to more important things.

"I really didn't mean for the tree decorating to take this long." He handed her the second strand of lights. "And I sure hope there's a female connection at the end of that strand you just put on."

"A *what?*"

He'd used the term without thinking, but he enjoyed the color seeping into her cheeks. He held up the plug he'd put into the outlet. "Male connection," he said. Then he reached for the end of the strand that she'd been putting on the tree. "Female connection." He plugged them firmly together.

She studied the connection. Eyes sparkling, she glanced at him. "Looks to me like that one you just plugged into mine is set up to be both."

"Well, yeah." He grinned. "Christmas-tree lights usually are made that way, now that you mention it. They swing both ways, I guess."

Although she was blushing, she didn't back down from the topic of conversation. "You know, I never understood the appeal of that."

"Me, neither." But he understood the appeal of a naked man and woman in the same room. He understood that very well right now, and he thought she did, too. He could kiss her and end the tree decoration activities. He was so tempted. "I say leave that bisexual stuff to the mollusks," he added.

Her gaze turned speculative. "Would you, now?"

Then he realized he'd just slipped and said something that didn't usually tumble out of an uneducated guy's mouth. He shrugged. "Learned that in the *Reader's Digest.*"

"Sure you did." Taking a deep breath, she broke eye contact in order to survey the bookshelves behind him. "Exactly how many of those have you read?"

So it would start now, he thought with a feeling of resignation. Him and his big mouth. She'd find out how thoroughly he'd educated himself and then she'd begin to urge him to better his circumstances. Well, he might as well get it over with.

"I've read nearly all of them," he said, admitting it the way a hardened criminal might confess to all the jobs he'd pulled. "Except for the volumes of Dickens I picked up last month. I'm still—"

"*All* of them?" Walking past him and over to the shelves, she began reading off names. "Emerson, Thoreau, Whitman, Dickinson." She glanced back at him before turning back to the shelves. "And this looks like the complete works of Shakespeare."

"It is."

"And my God, here are all the volumes of *The History of the Decline and Fall of the Roman Empire,* and Plato's *Republic* and the *Kama Sutra*..." She gazed at that book a little longer than necessary.

He began to wonder if he should explain why he had that one, in case she'd read it and was offended by its chauvinistic tone. "The original's kind of sexist, I admit, but I wanted to take a look, anyway. Back when it was written, women had no power. I've found updated versions that are probably better, in terms of making women equal partners in the lovemaking."

"I, um, haven't read any versions." She swallowed. "But I have read this." She stroked the spine of *Lady Chatterley's Lover.*

He thought about the premise of that book, the lady of the manor having an affair with the gardener. It struck a little too close to home.

Suzanne continued to wander the length of the bookshelves looking at his collection of psychology and history texts, and again at his books on economics. "I read some of these in college," she murmured almost to herself.

He watched her, hoping this really wasn't the beginning of the end, yet fearing that it could be. Although other women in the building had urged him to go back to college and better himself, they'd only been operating on a hunch that he had something on the ball and might be hiding his intelligence. He'd turned aside their suggestions easily enough.

They'd never seen his book collection, and he'd never admitted to anyone except his family that he'd virtually educated himself.

Suzanne probably wouldn't be able to resist trying to rescue a diamond in the rough. As much as he wanted to make love to her, he didn't want to endure a lecture about wasting his talents as a handyman in the process. This was his decision, and he needed her to respect it.

Finally she reached the end of the bookshelves and turned to him. "Is there any subject you haven't studied?"

"Astronomy," he admitted, "but I was thinking after the new year I might get into that."

Slowly she walked back to where he stood holding the second strand of Christmas lights. "When I gave you that little book ornament, I had no idea. I thought you might have inherited these from tenants who left them, and that maybe you'd started dipping into them for the heck of it. But it's obvious that you've gone about this very deliberately."

He waited for her to ask why. Why would a handyman want to know so many things? And with all that knowledge, why wouldn't he work toward a more prestigious job?

She gazed at him for a long time, but she didn't ask any questions at all. Instead, she held out her hand for a strand of lights. "Ready to start trimming the tree?"

"Sure." Maybe she'd wait until later, he thought. But he could almost guarantee that at some point she'd want to know why a man with a library of books and the equivalent of a university education was living in a basement apartment and fixing rusty pipes and broken electrical switches for a living.

9

GREG WAS FULL OF SURPRISES. As Suzanne went back to stringing lights on the tree, she kept thinking of Terri's question tonight at the gym. *What would you talk about after the sex?*

From the looks of Greg's bookshelf, Suzanne would run out of things to talk about long before Greg. Terri couldn't know about those books. Suzanne wondered if anybody in the building did.

She was dying to ask Greg if any of the other women had ever been down here, but discussing his previous affairs seemed tacky. Terri had said he was the soul of discretion, and Suzanne respected that. If the grapevine operated the way Terri had implied, then word about Greg's self-education project would have spread by now if even one of his lovers had seen these bookshelves and asked a question or two.

Suzanne began to believe she'd stumbled onto a secret. In that case, she would keep that secret without being asked.

As they finished the lights and started on the garland, Suzanne asked about the rest of Greg's family and discovered he had two younger brothers and a younger sister. Greg seemed in a hurry to get the trimming done and not inclined toward lengthy conversation about his mother and siblings, but he answered her questions, at least.

His impatience to finish the tree had become funny. She

knew exactly why he was pushing to complete it, but she wasn't about to abandon the chance to find out more about this intriguing man. Besides that, she wasn't capable of doing a slipshod job.

"I think that's a little too close to the other red ball." She unhooked an ornament that Greg had hung and repositioned it. "There. Much better. So, how old is your sister?"

He sounded as if he'd come to the end of his rope. "Twenty-three, and I'm so glad I didn't buy any more ornaments. This is taking w*aaaa*y too long."

"You can't hurry something like decorating a tree," she said with an inward smile. She stooped down to hang another ball in a bare spot and her muscles protested. Apparently they were starting to tighten up from her session at the gym.

By tomorrow she would really feel the effects of her workout. She could have used another herbal soak in her tub, but she hadn't wanted to take the time. Not tonight.

"Muscles still a little sore?" he asked nonchalantly.

She realized he must be watching her *very* closely. Her body warmed at the thought. "A little."

"Then I think we should quit. I could help you work out some of that stiffness if we—"

"We haven't put on everything you bought." She glanced down at the open boxes of ornaments. "Barely half."

"I can see I bought too much."

"Not really. You want it to look nice, don't you?"

"I want it to look done. Which it does."

"Okay, there." She hung one more ornament and stepped back to admire their work. The lights were well spaced and the garland circled the tree in even scallops of silver. No two ornaments of the same color hung beside each other. "Now, didn't I see a package of icicles some-where?"

"No."

"I did so." She turned just as he shoved something be-hind his back. "Come on, Greg. Unless you're worried about Matilda getting them?"

"She won't if they're up high enough. It's me. I hate ici-cles."

She walked toward him. "Then why did you buy some?"

He backed up a step. "Habit. Let's skip them."

"The tree won't look right without icicles." She moved closer, hand outstretched. "Give them to me and I'll do it if you don't want to."

"Nope." He backed up some more. "I would bet a mil-lion dollars that you put them on one at a time."

She regarded him in horror. "Don't tell me you throw it by the handful?"

"I would tonight." He kept retreating. "Tonight I'd throw it on with a pitchfork."

She could see where he was heading. Another step and he'd be inside his bedroom. "Greg, the tree's not finished without the icicles." She was a little impatient with herself for letting that bother her, but it was part of her personality to tie up all the loose ends before she left any project. Ap-parently even the promise of hot sex couldn't totally erase that tendency.

Very hot sex. Oh God, soon she was going to let him touch her again, kiss her again. Now that she knew more about him, those touches and kisses would take on a whole new meaning. He'd read the *Kama Sutra*—several ver-sions—and *Lady Chatterley's Lover*, and so many books on human sexuality that she'd lost count as she'd browsed his bookshelves.

For some reason, this fascinating man wanted to make love to her tonight, and she would certainly be happy for him to do that. In the process, though, she wasn't supposed to fall for him. Under no circumstances was she supposed to do that.

"Here's an idea." He backed through the doorway into shadow. "We can finish the tree tomorrow night."

Tomorrow night. Her heartbeat quickened. She hadn't thought that far ahead. When it came to temporary love affairs, she didn't know what the normal duration was. She'd never had a temporary love affair.

"Here's the deal, Suzanne. If you want these icicles, you'll have to come and get them. They'll be here, in the middle of the bed." He turned and walked into the bedroom. A soft plop announced that the icicles had landed.

When she realized the irony, she couldn't help laughing. Any woman who would walk into his bedroom, pick up a package of icicles from his bed and carry them back out so that she could finish decorating a Christmas tree would have to be an icicle, herself.

Jared had called her an anal-retentive ice queen, and she was here in Greg's apartment tonight to prove that she was nothing of the kind. So the tree would remain unfinished. She could live with that. Besides, he said they'd work on it tomorrow night. That not only satisfied her need to complete a project, it allowed for all sorts of other possibilities.

Heart pounding with anticipation, she started toward the bedroom. "Okay, you win," she said. "We can forget about the icicles for now." The room was still dark, and a delicious shiver ran up her spine. He would let her decide about the lights this time, too, apparently.

She was ready for a little bit of light—soft, delicate light. She hoped his lamp had a low setting. But whether it did or not, she vowed she wouldn't be the same timid woman who had demanded total darkness the night before. She didn't feel like that same woman, either. Spending an hour decorating a tree with an obviously aroused, impatient man had helped.

Even so, walking into the dark room and knowing he was there waiting for her made her knees weaken. Maybe this was why husbands carried brides over the threshold, because their legs turned to rubber as they contemplated what awaited them beyond that doorway.

As she stepped into the room, strong arms reached for her. He pulled her close and nudged the door closed with his foot, surrounding them in darkness once again. Oh, yes. She was ready for this. With a moan she wrapped her arms around his neck and surrendered to his kiss.

AT LAST. GREG'S KISS was filled with gratitude that she'd finally decided to give in and let him love her. Sure, he'd wanted to spend a little time in conversation so he could learn more about her, a little time in an activity like trimming the tree, but enough was enough. As for loving this woman, he might never get enough.

She tasted like heaven, but he'd waited too long to be able to pause and savor the lush territory of her mouth. Seconds into the kiss, he reached for the single pearl button of her cardigan. In no time he'd peeled the soft garment away and started on the button of her skirt.

He hadn't forgotten about the panty hose that he suspected she wore under that skirt, and he wanted to get rid of them early in the game. If he waited until desire had built to a fever pitch and his patience had deserted him completely, her panty hose might end up in tatters.

She'd pulled his T-shirt from the waistband of his jeans and slipped warm hands up his bare back, which he found tremendously encouraging. That and the mistletoe she'd brought made him think she wanted an active part in this adventure, after all. And yet she'd pulled away from his kiss earlier.

He needed to remember that. Even now, as her touch fed the ache in his groin, he needed to remember that and be careful. It didn't take much imagination to think of those hands stroking other parts of him in a caress he'd denied himself the night before. He wouldn't deny himself this time, but always, always, he had to be careful. Letting down his guard completely would be a mistake.

Unzipping the skirt, he pushed the supple suede over her hips and let the skirt fall to the floor as he cupped her bottom with eager hands. That's when he discovered that he'd been wrong. Instead of panty hose, she'd worn a lacy garter belt and stockings. His breath caught. He had a special weakness for a woman in a garter belt and stockings.

He'd told himself to expect that she'd want darkness again tonight. He'd decided that he might have to make love to her several times before he could hope to tap into the instinct that had urged her to place a red pillow on her white sofa and a red devil in the middle of her bed. Perhaps, although he hated to think of it, he never would find that inner sex kitten.

But a garter belt and stockings on a woman with legs like Suzanne's...now *that* was something that demanded visual appreciation. Slowly he lifted his mouth from hers. His voice rasped in the darkness. "What color?"

Her breath came quick and fast, like his. "Black." A pause. "Do you want to see?"

"Yes. Lord, yes. Can I?" He waited.

"Is your lamp...very bright?"

Thank God he'd prepared for this. "I have something better than the lamp. Wait right here." He stepped over to the bedside table and fumbled with the matches he'd put there earlier. It took him several tries before he managed to light the match because he was shaking so much.

A garter belt and stockings. Hot damn. And he would be able to see her tonight while they made love. He'd been going crazy trying to imagine her naked body, and now he wouldn't have to imagine anymore. He would know.

He heard rustling noises behind him as he worked to light the candles. "Don't take your garter belt off," he said. "I—"

"Don't worry. I won't."

Something in her voice was different, and as he touched a quivering flame to the candle's wick, he figured out what it was. Her voice sounded sultry. He thought he'd never get the second candle lit with the way he was trembling. So he wouldn't have to wait so long after all. Her hidden sensual streak was showing already.

He finally managed to get the candles burning. He turned, the match flame still wavering in his hand. The sight that greeted him nearly stopped his heart in midbeat. She'd taken off her boots and her sweater. That considerate move would have been enough to drive him thoroughly crazy, considering that her black garter belt matched a black bra that gave her enough cleavage to inspire his dreams for weeks.

But that wasn't all. She'd stretched out on the bed in that fantasy outfit, propping her head on her hand. She'd also opened the box of icicles and sprinkled them all over her. Candlelight sparkled on the silvery strands, and he thought of how much fun he was going to have taking them off...one at a time.

He yelped as the match burned his finger. Shaking it out, he dropped the spent match in a small dish he'd left on the night table for exactly that purpose. Burning his finger while staring at Suzanne hadn't made him look very cool and collected. He'd completely forgotten he was holding a match.

"Would you like me to kiss it and make it better?" she asked in that sultry voice that fried every circuit in his brain.

"With an offer like that, I might have to set a few more body parts on fire." He felt as if parts of him were about to spontaneously combust, anyway.

"Let me see that poor burned finger." Lying back on the pillow, she held her hand out to him.

He played along, even though the flame had barely nipped him. Sitting on the edge of the bed, he placed his hand in both of hers.

Holding his gaze, she brought his finger up to her mouth. "Poor baby." She kissed the tip with her full lips. Then, as he'd suspected she would, she began to suck his finger, curling her tongue around it and watching his expression as she imitated the very maneuver she'd offered him the night before.

His jeans became a tourniquet that resisted the natural expansion going on under the denim. Oh, man, he had to undress, and he needed two hands. He hated to put an end to her erotic demonstration, but if he didn't get his clothes off soon he'd be seriously dented.

"Hold that thought," he murmured as he eased his finger from her hot mouth. He stood and reached for the back of his T-shirt to pull it over his head. Then he remembered the mistletoe in his pocket. Pausing, he took it out and laid it on the nightstand near the candles.

Her gaze followed.

"I have some ideas for that mistletoe." He pulled off his T-shirt.

"So do I."

Oh, Lord. He'd pictured her turning sexy and seductive,

but he'd never imagined that her voice would become as smooth as fine whiskey. They'd spent way too much time on that tree, he thought as he pulled off his shoes and socks.

Or maybe not. Maybe she'd enjoyed making him wait. Maybe she was beginning to understand the extent of her power, awakening her inner temptress. Whatever the reason, he loved what was happening.

He looked into her eyes as he unfastened his jeans and shoved them down. "Now you can see what you do to me," he said.

Her eyes sparkled with obvious triumph as she took in his state of arousal. Then she glanced away and casually rearranged some of the icicles, letting them shiver down the inside of her black-stockinged thighs. "I've heard garter belts have that effect."

She was teasing him. He could hardly believe his good fortune as he watched the icicles catch the candlelight. Those lying against her thighs would be so much fun to lift away. "You had that effect long before I knew about the garter belt." He peeled off his briefs.

Her breath caught.

What a sweet, sweet sound. A sound to bolster a man's ego, if ever he'd heard one. He put a knee on the mattress and gazed at her. "Will I do, then?" he asked softly.

She met his gaze, and even in the pale light from the candles, he could see that her cheeks were rosy with excitement. Her lips were parted and her breasts rose in response to her rapid breathing. "You'll do," she said in that smoky voice. Then her lips curved. "Me."

His heart raced as he returned her saucy smile. The little red devil in her had come out to play. "I sure will, sweetheart. I sure as heck will. I'm only trying to decide where to start. You seem to be covered in icicles."

"You wouldn't let me put them on the tree, so—"

"I like them *much* better here." He captured several strands lying across the swell of her breasts and drew them back and forth over her bare skin. "Does that tickle?"

"Yes."

"Good." He swept the icicles aside and leaned down to run his tongue along the lace-trimmed edge of her bra.

"That...tickles...too."

"Even better." He drew back and surveyed his next target. A few icicles clung to her bra, and he pulled them away, making sure that he stroked her thoroughly in the process. From the sound of her breathing, he knew his touch was having the desired effect.

"And look." He gazed at the smooth, inviting skin of her belly. "More icicles." He removed them one by one, taking his time, trailing kisses over each area that he cleared of the silvery strands.

In response, her skin grew warm and flushed, and she began to quiver beneath him. "The icicles were a little joke," she said breathlessly. "I didn't realize that it would feel like...this...when you took them off."

"Do you like it?" Dipping his tongue in her navel, he picked icicles gently from her garter belt.

"Mmm." She trembled even more. "I do."

"Me, too." He picked up a strand that was draped over one of her long black garters and drew it back and forth over the tops of her thighs, above the sheer black nylons.

She moaned softly.

He shifted his attention to the icicles decorating her stocking-covered thighs and pulled them off slowly as he licked and nibbled his way to her knees. All the while he breathed in the wonderful aroma of arousal and savored all that awaited him.

At last the icicles were gone except one. He swirled it

back and forth over her knees before bringing it up her leg and dropping it deliberately between her thighs. "Whoops. Lost that one. Better get it back." He pretended to fumble for the icicle.

She gasped as his groping brought him in contact with the damp triangle between her legs.

"I've nearly found it." He ran his knuckles back and forth over the material. "Spread your thighs a little wider, so I can search."

"Greg..."

"Come on, now," he murmured. "You're the one who draped yourself in icicles. I think you want this."

With a soft moan of surrender, she parted her thighs.

Heart hammering, he slipped his fingers under the black silk. This time would be the beginning, not the ending, so he wouldn't draw it out like he had the night before.

"Tell me you want this," he said, his voice husky as he probed her moist heat.

"Yes," she whispered.

That single word made him tremble with longing. As he pushed in deep with two fingers, his thumb came to rest naturally on the exact place he wanted to caress.

She moaned again as he began.

Maintaining a gentle rhythm, he eased up beside her and saw that her eyes were closed. "Suzanne, look at me," he coaxed.

Her eyes flickered open, and they were dark with passion.

"It's so much better when I can see your eyes. So much better." He felt her tightening. "Good?"

She began to pant. "Yes."

"This is only a taste." He increased the rhythm. "An appetizer."

She looked as if she didn't believe him, as if she expected

no more than this. He would give her so much more before the night was over.

He smiled at her and fluttered his thumb faster yet. "We have all night, remember? Now come for me, Suzanne. Let go." He caressed her with a fraction more pressure, and she arched from the bed with a cry.

A rush of emotion took him by surprise. As he gathered her close and held her while she quaked in the aftermath of her climax, he tried to deny what that emotion was. But in his heart he knew.

SHE'D BEEN BOLD, and he'd responded to her boldness. At first she'd wondered if her usual shyness would ruin the moment, but he'd helped her through. She felt exhilarated knowing that for once in her sexual life, she'd been spontaneous.

Greg nuzzled her neck as he held her close in his arms. "I love that wild little sound you make when you come."

"What sort of sound?"

He leaned back to gaze into her eyes. "You don't know?"

Her cheeks warmed and she shook her head. Both times he'd given her an orgasm, she'd been too caught up in the earthquake that took over her body to think about the sounds she made.

"It's a cross between a cry and a moan. Unique. Very primitive. Extremely sexy. Nobody's ever mentioned it?"

"No." Not that Jared would have. He was always so involved in his own pleasure that she'd sometimes wondered if he took much notice of hers. Now that she thought about it, no man had ever lavished as much attention on her as Greg. They'd expected her to cooperate in whatever new position or location they'd wanted to try, but she'd felt more like an accessory than a cherished partner.

"Maybe that's because this is the first time you've made that sound." Greg looked pleased with the idea.

"Maybe."

"I plan to hear it again before long." He cupped her bottom and drew her close, so that his erection pressed against her belly. "I love this outfit."

"I'm glad." Her confidence grew with every compliment he gave her. She was ready to try another daring move, one she'd imagined as she'd dressed for tonight's rendezvous. She'd bought the bra and garter belt when she'd been with Jared and had never felt comfortable enough with him to wear it.

But Greg inspired her to take chances. She reached for the front clasp of the bra. "You might like this variation even better." She opened it with a flick of her manicured fingers. The black lace cups clung for a moment, before she deliberately pulled them back. "What do you think?"

His hungry eyes feasted for a long, long, time. Against her thigh, his penis quivered in response. "I think you're absolutely perfect," he said. Then he looked into her eyes. "Thank you."

"I think...that's my line." She traced his mouth with the tip of her finger. "Thank you for changing your mind. For deciding you...wanted me."

He shook his head. "I've always wanted you. I just didn't think..." He hesitated.

"Didn't think I was up to the challenge?" How quickly her confidence could evaporate.

"No!" He caught her chin and forced her to look at him. "No," he said again, more softly. "I wasn't sure *I* was."

"I'm no challenge, Greg."

"Now that's where you're wrong." Cupping her breast,

he eased her to her back. "You might be the biggest challenge I've ever faced in my life."

Before she could ask him what he meant, he kissed her, and after that she completely forgot the question.

10

GREG FILLED HIS HANDS with Suzanne's breasts, massaging her satin skin, fondling her taut nipples. And all the while he continued to kiss her until they were both breathless. At last he lifted his mouth from hers. "I wish I was twins so I could keep kissing your mouth and kiss you everywhere else at the same time."

"I'd go mad with pleasure."

"That's what I want." He nibbled his way down her throat and over her collarbone. "To drive you mad with pleasure. Out of your mind, so you'll make those wild little sounds again."

She gasped for breath. "You're off to a good start."

He reached one breast and drew a nipple greedily into his mouth.

She groaned. "A very good start. Oh, Greg. That feels so...delicious."

When she gripped the back of his head, transmitting her urgency, he sucked harder, and felt her quake. His hand slipped automatically downward, pulling her panties aside, sliding his fingers deep.

She arched against his hand, needing him.

Fierce joy surged through him at that silent admission that she wanted more. Tonight he would give her all she could take. With his fingers buried deep and his mouth at her breast, he felt almost as much a part of her as if they were joined completely. And he wanted that final joining soon. His groin ached for it. But this...this was so good.

Vibrating his fingers while keeping them inside her, he was able to feel the wave of her first contraction. Then he heard that sound, that wonderful sound she made as the contractions rolled past his fingers.

He stayed with her, his mouth at her breast and his fingers inside, until her body stopped humming and her wild cries ceased. Then he slowly released her breast and eased his fingers free.

When at last he moved upward to gaze into her eyes, glowing in the aftermath of her climax, he felt that dangerous emotion squeeze his heart again. If he fell in love, and she turned out to be like all the other women who had expected him to change his life, he was doomed.

"That was...incredible," she murmured.

He pushed his fear aside. This moment was too wonderful to waste on fear. "You are incredible." With gentle motions he finished removing her bra. "And this is why I love having light, so I can see how beautiful you look after you come."

"I thought..." Suddenly she looked very vulnerable. "I thought men liked making love in the light because they liked to ogle."

The only thing that kept him from chuckling was that vulnerable expression of hers, which told him that she wasn't making a joke. "I'll be honest. Once or twice I've been known to ogle."

He leaned down and touched his lips to hers. "But I know what you're talking about," he murmured, kissing her softly again. "You're talking about looking at a woman as if she's a collection of body parts instead of your lover, the person you've chosen to share this experience with." That's what he'd gathered from listening to women's complaints about men. Lifting his head, he studied her expression to see if what he'd said had helped.

Apparently it had. She had stars in her eyes again. "That's it," she said. "That's exactly it. And then I feel so—exposed."

"I don't want that." He stroked her breast tenderly as he watched her face. "I want you to feel well loved."

"Oh." She sighed a little as she said it. "I do."

Those two little words jolted him. Marriage ceremony words. Until now, Amelia had been the only woman he'd imagined saying them. Once Amelia had disappeared from his life, he'd thought about marriage in generalities, but never specifically related to one woman. And now, God help him, he was thinking exactly that about Suzanne.

So far it wasn't a fully formed thought. He'd be wise to kill it now, if he possibly could.

Then she reached down and curled her hand around his penis, and he lost all track of what he'd been worrying about. Tonight he had no worries. Suzanne was stroking him lovingly, and nothing mattered but that.

"I want you to feel well loved, too," she said. "Up to now it's been all about me."

"That's...okay." For some reason, he had trouble remembering how to talk when she created that cylinder-and-piston effect. He could barely remember his name. Thank heavens he'd relieved some of his pent-up tension the night before, or he wouldn't last five seconds. And he wanted to last a long, long time.

Her voice was as smooth as her hand motion. "Would you give me the mistletoe?"

Would he ever. Now, if he could only think of what he'd done with it.

"On the nightstand," she murmured.

Oh, yeah. But if he turned over to get it, she might lose her place. He didn't want that happening.

"On second thought, let me get it," she said.

He didn't want that, either. If only the mistletoe could get its own self over here, so she could make whatever naughty use of it she had in mind. The concept made him delirious with anticipation, but somebody had to get the darned mistletoe.

"Hold still," she said. Keeping a firm grip on him, she slid her leg over his. Without breaking contact, she guided him to his back and moved astride his thighs. In the process she winced.

"Something hurts," he said.

"Too much time on the thigh machine. But never mind."

He stoked her inner thighs. "Let me massage—"

"Nope." She grabbed a wrist in each hand. "I know what would happen if you started massaging me there."

"But I—"

"Later." She glanced at the night table. "Is that why you have massage oil over there?"

"Yes."

"It's a very nice thought," she said softly. "But it's my turn, and I want you to keep your hands to yourself. Can you do that?"

"I don't know."

"If you don't know, then I can't let go of your wrists, and if I can't let go of your wrists, then I can't..." She glanced at his ramrod-straight penis.

That made things easy. "I promise," he said.

"Okay, then." As if he were a naughty boy she'd had to reprimand, she gave him the most adorable look of warning as she released his wrists. Then her fingers slid around him again, making him sigh with pleasure.

He wondered if she'd forgotten the mistletoe, not that he

cared. What she was doing was wonderful, fabulous. She was driving him slowly crazy with her stroking and tickling until he groaned from the sheer pleasure of it.

But he had trouble remembering his promise not to touch her when her breasts hovered tantalizingly within reach. They were so beautiful, so silky, so full. They beckoned him, called to him, tortured him with their proximity. At last he reached to cup them in his hands.

"Greg."

Obediently he lowered his hands. He was glad to let her be in charge. Overjoyed. Then she leaned toward the night-stand to pick up the mistletoe, and her breasts swayed temptingly close to his mouth. He lifted his head and captured one pouting nipple.

With a siren's smile, she eased her breast away from his mouth.

"But you said no hands." He sounded like a little kid denied his lollipop, which was sort of the way he felt. He wanted it all. "That was my mouth, not my hand."

"No mouth, either," she murmured, picking up the mistletoe and bracing her hands on either side of his head. "Now lie still."

"I don't know if that's humanly possible."

"Try."

He looked into her eyes and saw the gleam of sexual adventure there. This was the Suzanne he'd been looking for, and apparently he'd found her.

She copied his earlier work with the mistletoe, trailing it over his face and kissing him everywhere the mistletoe touched. But she was far more thorough than he'd been.

Smoothing the mistletoe around his ear, she leaned down to whisper into it. "Do you like that?"

He loved it. Few women had ever discovered it was one of his most potent erogenous zones. "Yes."

She ran her tongue around the outer part and gently nipped his earlobe. "That?"

He was in heaven. "Yes."

Then she flicked her warm tongue inside his ear and he nearly came unglued. Only one other place on his body was that sensitive, and he had a feeling she'd get to that place before long.

"I think you *really* like that," she said.

He was having trouble breathing. "Uh-huh." And wouldn't you know, she treated his other ear to the same warm, wet stimulation. He was trembling before she was finished, and he needed to grab...something. He clutched her bottom.

"No," she murmured, her breath tickling his damp ear.

"I have to...hold on to something."

"Then grab the sheet."

He took a handful in each fist, and he definitely needed to once she started moving the mistletoe down his body. He squeezed the life out of those sheets as she licked his nipples. The path down to his naval required even more self-control. He braced himself for the final assault.

But no, she bypassed home base and slid down to work him over from the toes up. He'd thought his ears were the second most sensitive body part, but oh, Lord, when she sucked his toes he nearly climaxed.

And he'd begun to whimper. At first he couldn't figure out where that funny sound was coming from, and then while she was licking the backs of his knees he realized he was making noises like a puppy eager for supper. Besides that, he was starting to twitch.

When she kissed the inside of his thighs, he whimpered and twitched at the same time. Then she moved higher, and he discovered neither his ears nor his toes were the second most sensitive body part. That honor belonged to the family jewels. His chest heaved and he gritted his teeth, not wanting to climax and end this miraculous adventure.

At last she stroked the mistletoe up the shaft of his penis. Her mouth followed. Oh, did it ever follow. She understood the full extent of her power, and she was using it. He allowed the ecstasy to last as long as he dared, but too soon he was forced to bury his fingers in her hair and pull her gently back to his mouth for a long, deep kiss.

Still kissing her, he rolled her to her back and reached for the drawer handle on the nightstand. He was coming to the end of his endurance, and he didn't want that to happen before he'd made love to a woman wearing nothing but a garter belt and stockings. He'd have to ruin her panties by ripping them, but how he would love buying her a new pair and remembering why he'd had to replace them.

Once he had the condom in his hand, he was forced to end the kiss so he could concentrate on getting it on.

She was breathing as hard as he was. "Can I help?"

He looked into her passion-darkened eyes as he gulped for air. "If you touch me there again, even for a second, I'm done for."

"You've been mistletoed."

"Yeah." His laugh was breathless with anticipation as he rolled the condom into place. "I sure have. Completely mistletoed." He gazed down at her. "And now I want the ending to my fantasy." He gripped the delicate fabric of her panties right where they were the dampest. In one quick motion he ripped them apart.

She gasped, and excitement flared in her eyes. "You tore my underwear!"

"Exactly." And with one firm thrust he was where he needed to be, and it felt as perfect as he'd thought it would. Heart pounding, he stayed very still, enjoying the warmth, the tightness, the sweet reality of being linked so intimately with her.

Her eyes glowed as she slid her hands up his back and clutched his shoulders. "I can't believe you tore my underwear."

"You wanted me to," he whispered.

She nodded.

"Is there anything I haven't done that you wanted?"

"Only what's coming next," she murmured.

"Good." He leaned down and kissed her full on the mouth. Then he lifted his lips a fraction. "But before that, I want to ogle." He raised up so that he could look into her eyes. "Just a little."

She smiled. "Okay." As if in surrender, she let go of his shoulders and put both arms over her head.

Heart racing, he flattened his hands on either side of her, straightened his arms and gazed down at the arousing sight of Suzanne lying beneath him, her breasts uncovered and quivering with each breath. Below that, where he was buried deep within her, were the tattered remnants of her panties and that sexy black garter belt still circling her hips, the garters fastened to smooth black stockings. Perfect.

He cleared the huskiness from his throat. "Wrap your legs around me." Then he remembered her encounter with the thigh machine. "Unless that would hurt you."

"It's only a twinge." She wrapped her legs securely around his hips, opening herself even more.

His pulse quickened as her legs tightened around him. He eased a little more upright and at last couldn't help himself. He wanted the entire fantasy. Sliding his hands under her bottom, he lifted her hips as he rose to a kneeling position. He held her there as he began a slow, rhythmic thrusting.

Lord forgive him, but he was definitely ogling now.

With Suzanne stretched out in front of him, arms flung over her head, breasts jiggling with every deliberate thrust, he was living the most erotic dream he could have imagined. Yes, he was ogling, and she didn't seem to mind a bit. Her gaze was fixed on his, and it was filled with pure seduction.

He shouldn't hold this position long, he told himself, even as the look in her eyes urged him to increase the pace. He should remember that she might not be able to find satisfaction in this position. Not every woman could. Ah, but he hated to stop. This was so good. So very good.

As he pumped faster, her lips parted and her chin lifted a fraction. He would almost swear that she was getting close. She reached back and got a grip on the iron scrollwork behind her head. The picture kept getting better and better, he thought.

Then she lifted her hips a little more and shifted the angle slightly. "Now," she whispered.

"You can?"

"Oh, yes." Her eyes darkened. "Oh...*yes.*" With that special cry of hers, she arched her neck as the spasms overtook her.

He needed nothing more than that. He came in a hot flood of release that left him dazed and gasping. As his sanity gradually returned, a powerful realization came with it. She'd surpassed his wildest dreams in bed, and she was all that he'd hoped for out of bed, too. She was all he'd ever wanted in a lover, in a partner, in a mate. If she didn't want to change him and make him into someone more acceptable for her, he'd found the woman he wanted to marry.

TIME TO LEAVE NOW, Suzanne decided as she and Greg lay in his bed recovering slowly from their lovemaking. Greg cuddled after sex better than any man she'd known. And it scared her to death.

Her heart told her she'd found the perfect guy, and yet she dared not trust it. Her brain knew that she might not be thinking clearly, for one thing. She'd recently been through a bad breakup, and she might think anybody who gave her three orgasms in one night was perfect.

The biggest reason she couldn't listen to her heart, though, was Greg himself. He had a hobby of comforting women after bad breakups. Sure, he enjoyed the process—anyone could see that—but Terri had said right from the start that Greg didn't want to tie himself down.

The way Terri put it, Greg understood that his lifestyle wouldn't mesh with that of any of the professional women in this building. Suzanne wasn't so sure about that. Greg was certainly educated enough to hold his own. Yet maybe he was the kind of guy who didn't feel comfortable in a white-collar world and wouldn't like having a wife who lived in that world, either.

A wife. She'd made that leap in a heck of a hurry. Greg hadn't even suggested they might become a steady couple let alone partners for life.

She needed to get out of this apartment and escape the seductive influences here before she said or did something that was totally inappropriate. So they'd had good sex. Great sex, from her standpoint. Greg was probably used to that. For all she knew, he'd had lots better.

On that depressing note, she started to ease herself out of his arms. "I think I'd better go back to my place."

His arms tightened around her. "Don't go yet," he murmured. His eyes were closed, and he sounded sleepy, and she didn't blame him. He'd had a busy night.

"We both have to work tomorrow," she said.

"Sleep here."

"No, I can't do that. I'd rather nobody saw me coming out of your apartment early in the morning."

He opened his eyes, but he made no comment. From the way he was looking at her, she wondered if she'd hurt his feelings.

The longer the silence stretched, the more she believed she had hurt his feelings. "Greg, shouldn't we be concerned about your job? You could lose it if anyone found out you'd been involved with one of the tenants."

He continued to gaze at her. "Is that the reason you don't want to stay?"

"That's part of the reason," she answered honestly. "The other part is that I'd rather not have people gossiping about me, either."

"Because you wouldn't want anyone to know that you spent the night with the janitor?"

She propped herself up on one elbow. "That is *not* the reason! How you make your living has nothing whatsoever to do with it. I happen to value my privacy, that's all."

He searched her expression as if looking for any indication that she wasn't telling the truth.

Someone had hurt him, she realized. Some woman had treated him with contempt because of his job. She wondered if it was anyone in the building. If so, it was a miracle that he'd continue to help out depressed female tenants.

She leaned down and kissed him tenderly. Then she looked into his eyes. "If you think I want to leave because I'm ashamed of having made love to you, the maintenance man in my apartment building, that's only because you don't know me well enough."

Some of the tension around his eyes relaxed. "Then why do you want to go?"

"I could put your job in jeopardy."

"I understand that. But you also said you didn't want to

be gossiped about. That sounds as if you're less than proud of being with me."

She caressed his cheek as she gazed into his eyes. "You're right, it does sound that way, and the truth is, I really don't give a damn about whether people gossip about me. I threw that out so I wouldn't have to tell you the real reason."

"Which is?"

She took a deep breath. "I need some space. What's happened here tonight has been the most amazing sex of my life. Now, you probably hear that all the time."

"No, I—"

She laid a finger over his lips. "It's okay." She brushed her finger over his lower lip. "You don't have to humor me by saying it was the most amazing *you've* ever had. I don't need that."

His glance sharpened. "Not even if it's true?"

She thought of how Terri had described him. He knew all the right things to say to make a woman feel cherished. Of course he'd say this now. He was a sweet man, even if he wasn't into commitment. Maybe that was his destiny, to spread sunshine among many women instead of limiting himself to only one. He certainly had the talent for that role.

She managed a smile. "Give me some time to get my act together," she said.

"What's wrong with your act?"

"I keep having the crazy feeling that I'm falling in love with you," she said. "There. That should be enough to scare you to death." This time, as she slipped out of bed, he didn't try to stop her.

From the expression on his face, she decided that he was more than scared. He was terrified.

Her heart felt like lead as she gathered her clothes and headed for the door. "Don't worry," she said. "I promise I won't be a problem for you." Then she left. After her startling announcement, she didn't expect to be invited back.

11

HOURS LATER, the candles had sputtered out and Greg still wasn't sure what to do about Suzanne. Although he was thrilled that she might be falling in love with him, *she* didn't seem thrilled at all. She'd acted as if that wasn't an acceptable outcome of their relationship.

Yet why not? She'd said that his job didn't bother her in the least. Maybe he was a fool to believe that, but she'd looked totally sincere when she'd said it. Of course, all that hot sex might have impaired his judgment. *Might?* Hell, he could bet on it.

One thing was clear—whatever happened next in their relationship would be up to him. She'd left saying she wouldn't be a "problem" for him. That could be girl-speak for *I don't want you to be a problem for me.* But he would never know if he didn't test it.

And he would most definitely test it. Sure, he was taking the chance of being slammed to the mat if he discovered that Suzanne was indeed a snob who didn't want to be seen with a maintenance man. Although she hadn't immediately started questioning him about his future plans after discovering he was very well read, she still had time to do that, too.

Anyone could see that he was heading into dangerous territory if he pursued her. But after the way she'd made love to him tonight, he knew without a doubt that she was worth it.

IN EVERY ROMANCE NOVEL Suzanne had ever read, once the heroine thought she'd lost the hero for good, she spent a sleepless night grieving over it. Suzanne slept like a log, which might have had to do with those three fantastic orgasms Greg had given her.

When her alarm buzzed the next morning, however, misery set in with a vengeance. After only two nights in Greg's arms, she was hooked. She couldn't imagine how she'd survive without his kisses and his talented caress. She'd miss his conversation, his gentleness, even his *cat*, for heaven's sake. And—if she were totally honest with herself—she'd miss his significant body parts.

He hadn't been the only one ogling during their interlude. For the first time in her life she'd discovered the joy of ogling, female style. There was no other way to say it. Greg had the most beautiful penis she'd ever seen. And she would never, ever, see it again. *That* was worth crying over.

She shouldn't have told him she might be falling in love. That was stupid, stupid, stupid. But he'd looked so upset at the idea that she was ashamed of being with him because of his job, that she'd had to put those fears to rest. Maybe some other woman had dissed his choice of occupation, but Suzanne couldn't let him think that she was that type of person.

Even so, there must have been a million different ways she could have made a graceful exit without admitting that she was falling in love, for pity's sake. She could have pretended that she felt cramps coming on, for example, or that she was expecting an early-morning call from her mother. Anything but the truth.

A little white lie would have allowed her the space she needed to get a grip on herself. A little white lie would have meant that she could go back to see Greg again and enjoy more of what she craved.

But no, she'd had to tell the truth. She looked at her little red devil through brimming eyes. "It's all your fault!" She encompassed the entire mess in that statement, beginning with the impulse that had sent her down to Greg's apartment in the first place. She wasn't sure what had spawned that impulse, but she'd be happy to blame it on the devil.

Oh, well. Time to suck it up and get on with her life. She'd had a wonderful time for two fantastic nights, and discovered that she could be sexually adventurous, after all. If she had a bad feeling that Greg was the only person who inspired that kind of behavior, she hoped that she was wrong. She hated to think that she'd never be that uninhibited again.

Climbing out of bed, she discovered a new reason to be miserable. She could hardly walk. Most of it had to do with the gym and that blasted thigh machine, but some of it, she acknowledged as warmth coursed through her, was due to the wild sex she'd had in Greg's apartment.

A hot shower helped loosen her tight muscles. Coffee and a bagel made her feel marginally more human, but every time she looked at her little Christmas tree, she wanted to cry. Funny, but not having Jared around hadn't affected her Christmas spirit at all, but the prospect of not having Greg around had smashed her Christmas spirit to smithereens.

She also dreaded going downstairs to meet Terri this morning. They always took the same bus to work. If Suzanne didn't show up in the lobby at the regular time, Terri would come up to fetch her, so avoiding her wasn't an option. There would be more questions about Greg, though, and fielding them would not be easy.

At last she had no choice but to put on her boots and her

wool coat, sling the long strap of her leather briefcase over her shoulder and leave the safety of her apartment. That's when she saw the note lying on the carpet, a note that someone obviously had slipped under her door while she had been sleeping.

Her briefcase dropped to the floor as she stared at the note, her heart pounding. Without looking, she knew the note was from Greg. In the eighteen months she'd lived in this apartment, no one had ever slipped a note under her door. It definitely wasn't Terri's style to do something that subtle. Terri either called or came to see her.

But Greg *was* the type to write her a note. Because he was so considerate, he'd probably regretted not saying something soothing before she'd left his apartment. Once he recovered from the shock of her statement, he probably decided that he needed to do what he could to boost up her feelings—from a safe distance, of course, now that she'd announced that she might be falling for him.

She didn't want to read the note. Yet if she put it off until tonight, she'd spend the whole day wondering exactly what he'd said. So she'd read it quickly and then go straight down to meet Terri. She didn't have time for anything more, anyway. If she was tempted to call him after reading the note, she wouldn't be able to, and that was a good thing.

She picked up the folded sheet of paper. There was nothing unusual about it—a white, eight-and-a-half-by-eleven sheet, unlined, folded in half. She held her breath, and unfolded it. He'd printed in block letters:

Dear Suzanne,
Forgive me for not responding to what you said last night before you left. You caught me by surprise. Please don't ever think that you could be a "problem"

for me. I feel lucky to have you in my life, for however long that turns out to be. I'm not ready for our time together to be over. If you do want to end it, leave me a message and I'll understand. But if you're willing to see me again, I'd like to take you to a special little place for dinner tonight. It's nothing fancy, just a neighborhood pub where my friends and I hang out. Unless I hear from you, I'll be at your door by six.

Greg.

She read and reread the note. He wanted to take her out. She couldn't imagine why, but the fact remained that he wasn't through with her, after all. He wanted to take her out to dinner, apparently to meet his friends.

As with the books lining the wall of his apartment, and his cat, she suspected that this pub where he met his friends wasn't something he allowed everyone to know about him. She doubted seriously that Terri had the slightest idea that Greg met friends at a neighborhood pub from time to time. Therefore, she couldn't say a word to Terri about this.

Her doorbell buzzed, making her jump. Speaking of Terri, that would be her, wondering why on earth Suzanne wasn't down in the lobby ready to head for the bus stop. Suzanne was the most punctual person Terri knew, or at least that's what she'd always said.

Folding the note and tucking it in the pocket of her coat, Suzanne picked up her briefcase and opened the door.

Sure enough, Terri stood there looking worried. "Are you okay? I—"

"Crippled from the thigh monster, but otherwise fine," Suzanne said. "I was on my way down. Let's go or we'll be late."

"You don't look so crippled," Terri said as they dashed

for the elevator that had just stopped at her floor. "I've never seen you look more alive and happy."

"Must be all that exercise." She ducked into the elevator and held the button down so the door wouldn't close on Terri.

Terri looked as if she wanted to comment, but Jennifer, who lived on Suzanne's floor, had stepped into the elevator with them.

"You do look good, Suzanne," Jennifer said. "Did Terri finally talk you into joining the gym?"

"'Fraid so." Suzanne remembered that Jennifer had been the one who'd clued Terri in about Greg. So Jennifer had...no, she didn't want to go there. "If one of these days you see me crawling toward the elevator, I'd appreciate it if you'd help me make it up to my floor. I've never seen such torture machines as they have in that gym."

"You're going to thank me," Terri said as the elevator door slid open and they stepped out into the lobby. "There's nothing like being in shape to give a girl confidence."

"Unless it's a hot look from a guy like him," Jennifer said in an undertone.

Because Suzanne was the last one out of the elevator, she didn't realize that Jennifer was talking about Greg until a moment later, when she spotted him on a ladder tinkering with a smoke alarm on the far side of the lobby.

Her pulse skyrocketed at the sight of those long, lean legs, that muscled torso, those sinewy arms. Mere hours ago he'd been naked, holding her garter-covered hips and thrusting deep while his green eyes glowed with pleasure. She knew the pattern his chest hair created as it swirled around his nipples and traced a line downward to the thicket of hair between his thighs. Candlelight had caught the sheen of perspiration on his skin as he'd pumped faster, faster, faster.

Jennifer might know those intimate details about Greg, too, but Suzanne couldn't think about that now.

"Hey, Greg," Terri called across the lobby. "How's it going?"

Greg glanced over his shoulder. His gaze swept all three women, and his smile held no trace of uneasiness. "What's up, Terri? Hi there, Suzanne, Jennifer."

"Hi, Greg," Jennifer said. "Glad to see you're keeping those smoke alarms working."

"You bet," Greg said. "I don't plan on any of us going up in flames."

Except me, Suzanne thought, *if you take me to bed again tonight.* She needed to say something breezy, too, as the other two women had, but her throat felt as tight as her aching thighs. "Don't fall off the ladder, now," she said. *Don't fall off the ladder? What kind of lame remark was that?*

Greg didn't seem to notice how stupid she sounded. "I'll try not to," he said. Then he smiled again, and that smile seemed to be aimed right at her. "I wouldn't be much good for anything if I did that."

She could feel the heat in her cheeks and knew she must be blushing. "Right," she said.

"See you, Greg," Jennifer said. "My cab's out there." She glanced at Terri and Suzanne. "You two want to share?"

"That's okay," Terri said quickly. "Thanks, but your office isn't that close to ours. The bus is perfect for us."

"Perfect," Suzanne said. "Bye, Greg." She didn't look at either Jennifer or Terri as she charged out the revolving door to the street. Cold air had never felt so good.

"Wait for me, toots." Terri came hurrying up beside her, her boots crunching on the snowy sidewalk. "Wow." Her breath came out in clouds. "Good thing Greg's fixing that smoke alarm. The sparks shooting between you guys might set the place on fire."

"I don't know what you mean." Suzanne came to the bus stop and was forced to pause. Despite her sore muscles, she felt as if she could walk straight downtown, no problem.

Terri grinned. "Yeah, you do. And I'm happy for you. It's good to know I did the right thing, suggesting Greg. He's good medicine."

Suzanne drew the sharp, cold air into her lungs and tried to breathe normally. She couldn't keep her jealous thoughts about Jennifer at bay any longer. "Good medicine for Jennifer, too, I guess."

Terri reached over with one gloved hand and squeezed Suzanne's arm. "It doesn't matter, does it? This is your turn."

The churning in Suzanne's stomach grew worse as she thought about Jennifer, a tall, leggy brunette who worked as a fashion designer. No doubt Jennifer was way more exciting in bed than a financial analyst could ever dream of being. "She told you she'd slept with him?" She was a glutton for punishment.

"Yeah," Terri said. "But don't think about that. Remember, this is a temporary thing, anyway. Have fun. Don't get too attached, and just have fun."

Suzanne forced a smile. "Of course."

Terri studied her. "Oh, hell. You are getting attached, aren't you? Look, that's not a good idea. He's supposed to be your rebound man, remember?"

"I'm not attached," Suzanne said.

Terri sighed. "You are, and I should have known that was one of the dangers with you. You never have understood the concept of a casual affair. But I thought, considering he's a handyman, that you'd keep your emotional distance."

"I will! I mean, I am keeping my emotional distance." She decided not to argue with Terri about the snobbery thing. That would only confirm Terri's suspicion that there was a problem. Which there was.

"You really need to leave your heart out of this, Suzanne. Because no matter how much he seems to be involved, he'll eventually move on. And you may not think so now, but that's exactly what you want him to do."

"Absolutely." But of course she wanted nothing of the kind.

"Give it time and you'll see what I mean."

Suzanne nodded, although she didn't believe a word of it. With every minute that passed, she was falling deeper in love with the handyman.

MATILDA ALWAYS KNEW when Greg was preparing to leave, and she usually acted as if she could talk him out of it. Tonight she made a pest of herself by winding herself between his legs in an endless figure eight and meowing plaintively while he dressed.

"I'll be back," Greg promised. "We'll both be back." At least he hoped he and Suzanne would finish the evening together. Taking her to Jerry's Dogs and Suds was quite a trial by fire, but he had to know if a few hours in the company of his blue-collar friends would make her start questioning his lifestyle.

Yesterday he'd thought about skipping the weekly darts tournament so he could spend more time alone with Suzanne, but now he'd decided that the timing couldn't be better. He was falling fast for this vulnerable woman with her deeply sensuous nature. For some reason, she'd felt safe enough to reveal her true self to him, and he was captivated.

But they had no future if she couldn't accept *his* true self, a guy who wanted a simple job and unpretentious friends. Just because he loved to read and learn new things didn't mean he had any interest in joining the rat race. If she would end up nagging him about making something of himself instead of accepting him the way he was, then he might as well find out now so he could start cutting his losses.

He'd deliberately dressed down for this date, but even the long-sleeved flannel shirt seemed like too much of a statement, as if he wanted to impress her. Exactly the opposite. But the temperature had dropped a few more degrees, and a T-shirt wasn't going to do the trick, even with the down jacket he planned to wear. And instead of his trusty sneakers, he'd need to put on his hiking boots to better handle the snow and slush.

They'd be taking the bus. He had a truck parked in the building's underground garage, but he didn't normally drive it to the pub and he wasn't about to drive it now because Suzanne was going with him. She needed to get a realistic picture of the way he liked to live. If she could deal with that, then maybe they had a good thing going.

As he sat down on the bed and leaned over to lace up his hiking boots, Matilda put her front paws on his knee and meowed right in his face.

He cupped a hand behind her head and rubbed the base of her ears with a thumb and forefinger. "This is important, Matilda. I have to find out if Suzanne is going to become a permanent fixture around here or if she's just a passing fancy."

Putting it into words like that made his stomach churn. He was already more entangled with Suzanne than he wanted to admit, and pushing her out of his heart wasn't going to be easy.

As he continued to massage Matilda's head, she purred and closed her eyes.

"Wish me luck, Matilda," he murmured.

SUZANNE CHANGED CLOTHES four times. If it hadn't been nearly six o'clock, she might have changed again. The whole problem was Jennifer. Before being confronted with Jennifer, Suzanne had shoved Greg's "other women" into a mental closet and they'd pretty much stayed there until this morning.

Now thoughts of Jennifer were driving her crazy. Jennifer worked in a very creative field and she dressed with flair and imagination. Suzanne had spent an embarrassing amount of time during the day reviewing her closet and had concluded that she owned nothing that spoke of flair and imagination.

She might have used her lunch hour to shop, except she'd spent so much time thinking about her wardrobe, she was forced to eat at her desk so that she could finish a report that was due that afternoon. Consequently she'd faced her closet at five twenty-five praying for a miracle, hoping she'd forgotten something that she'd bought on a whim and then hung out of sight.

What a dreamer. She never bought anything on a whim and she usually opted for black. There was enough damn black in her closet to dress a church full of mourners. She'd worn one of her few exceptions, the red twinset, the night before.

Worse than that, she had almost nothing appropriate for a night at a cute little pub. Her status-conscious dates hadn't taken her to places like that, so she had dressy outfits, work outfits and exercise outfits.

Except for one thing. As a last resort, she'd put it on, and now she had to go with it because Greg could be arriving any minute.

Her father had given her the sweater at least six or seven years ago. He'd bought it during a skiing trip, and it had little images of a skier knit into the pattern. Suzanne had never skied in her life and wearing the sweater seemed like false advertisement, so she hadn't ever put it on.

Except for the skiers, the sweater's red-and-gold pattern reminded Suzanne of a favorite blanket she'd taken to Girl Scout camp when she was ten. A spark from the campfire had burned a big hole in it and her mother had convinced her to throw it away. She'd often wondered if her dad had remembered that blanket and had bought her the sweater because of it.

Once, she'd taken the sweater out of a bottom drawer and shown it to Jared to get his reaction. He'd called it "hokey" and suggested she give it to charity. She probably should have but instead she'd tucked it back in her bottom drawer.

Dressed in that sweater and her tried-and-true black wool slacks and snow boots, she felt completely without flair. No wonder Greg had hesitated taking her to bed that first night, considering he had someone like Jennifer to compare her with. Even her underwear was boring. The garter belt and matching bra was as exciting as it got with her.

The doorbell buzzed, and her heart kicked into high gear. She took a deep breath and reminded herself to play it cool. Terri might be wrong about Greg's suitability, but she was probably right that he would move on soon. Emotional distance was a very good idea.

The minute she opened the door and saw him standing there looking like the most gorgeous woodsman she could imagine, her emotional distance evaporated. His soft flannel shirt looked perfect for cuddling in front of the fire in that Wisconsin cottage he dreamed of owning someday. Unwise though it might be, she wanted this man, wanted him with a fierce ache that wouldn't be tamped down.

"That's a great sweater," he said.

She'd been so caught up in admiring how manly he looked in his green plaid shirt that she'd forgotten to be embarrassed about the sweater. "It's okay," she said, stepping back so that he could come inside. "You didn't have to say that. At least it'll be warm."

"You don't like it?" he asked.

She hesitated, thinking of Jennifer. *To hell with it.* "Yes, I do," she said. "My dad got it for me and it reminds me of my childhood. But it's a sweater you'd wear on a skiing vacation, and I don't even ski."

"So? Is there a law against wearing a sweater like that if you don't ski?"

"I guess not." Feeling much better than she had five minutes ago, she thought about how comforting it was to be with someone who didn't worry about such things. Come to think of it, he might not have cared whether Jennifer had fashion flair or not.

"I brought you something." He pulled a flat box out from under his arm. It was wrapped in red and green Christmas paper and tied with a silver bow.

"A Christmas present?" She took the box.

"Not exactly, although you did bring me and Matilda those things last night."

She felt her cheeks grow warm as she remembered the mistletoe she'd put at the bottom of that gift bag, and how she'd used it later. "That wasn't really a—"

"Well, this isn't either. But the gift-wrap department automatically did it up that way, and I decided to go with it."

She opened the package carefully, the way she did every package, trying her best not to rip the paper. When she heard him chuckle, she glanced up. "What?"

"I'm just enjoying watching you open it."

"Pretty anal, huh? But the paper is so pretty, and I—"

"I wouldn't have you do it any other way."

She looked into his eyes and her heart lurched. There was definitely something warm and adoring about the way he was gazing at her. Maybe he'd perfected that particular expression because he knew it made women feel cherished. If so, it worked. She could wallow in that warmth all night.

Forcing herself to break eye contact, she went back to opening the package. At last she lifted the lid to the box, moved aside the tissue paper, and found a pair of black silk panties underneath. Their sexual adventures from the night before tumbled over her like a breaking wave, making her ears buzz and her chest tight.

"I had to guess at the size." His gentle voice didn't seem to fit with the chaos he'd caused by giving her this sexual reminder. "Suzanne, are you okay?"

She nodded, afraid to look at him for fear he'd see the lust in her eyes. She didn't want to go to dinner. All she wanted was to rip off his clothes and hers and repeat everything they'd done the night before.

"They might not be exactly like your other ones." He sounded worried. "There's a gift receipt in there, so you can exchange them if you want. The salesclerk thought that would be a good idea. She said that guys don't always correctly guess a woman's—"

"They're perfect." She swallowed and lifted her gaze to his, her heart pounding. "Are you..." She paused and cleared her throat. "Are you sure you want to go to dinner right away?"

12

WHEN GREG SAW the seductive gleam in Suzanne's blue eyes, he forgot to breathe. He'd been struggling to contain his own lust ever since she'd closed the door and created the privacy to do...anything they chose. Oh, Lord. His body throbbed and his head spun. They had plans, but there was no schedule. None at all.

He wasn't sure who dropped what first, but suddenly his coat hit the floor along with the box holding her new panties. Then they jumped each other—kissing and fumbling with buttons and zippers. There were no words, only moans and urgent caresses.

Her sweater came off in a jiffy and her bra was no challenge, either. But they had to unfasten the cuffs of his shirt and some of the buttons down the front before they could pull it over his head to join the growing pile of clothes on the floor. She wrestled with his jeans and he worked on her slacks as they moved toward the sofa. Soon both were down around their knees, giving them plenty of access but no mobility.

"Boots," she said, gasping. "We have to—"

"I know." But he didn't want to stop kissing her and stroking her hot, moist body, so he returned his tongue to her mouth as he pulled her down to the sofa. But the slacks she still wore kept her from spreading her legs the way he wanted, and his hiking boots felt like a pair of concrete overshoes.

At last he wrenched his mouth from hers to take care of the last impediments. Panting like a winded runner, he reached past his aching erection and fumbled with his bootlaces as he gave her a ragged command to do likewise. After what seemed like forever, they were both naked and rolling together on the sofa. He didn't think they'd spend much time on foreplay, not with the way she was spreading her thighs and clutching his bottom.

He managed to stop kissing her for a split second. "Condoms?"

A short, heated silence was followed by her anguished wail. "I don't have any! Don't you?"

"No!"

She looked absolutely frantic. "Oh, Greg! I really need—"

"And you'll get, too." He started to slide south to give her what she needed. At least one of them could go to dinner happy.

She cupped the back of his head, stopping his progress. "No. That's not fair."

He glanced up at her. "Let me love you."

Her eyes smoldered with unchecked passion. "Then we'll love each other. Together," she murmured.

He could hardly believe this was the same woman who had insisted on making love in the dark two nights before. Here they were under bright lights in the middle of her living room, and if she was suggesting what he thought she was suggesting, she'd lost nearly all her inhibitions.

"Let me get on top." Her voice was as bold as her glance.

"Are you suggesting what I think you are?"

Her lips parted and her breath came in quick little spurts. She was trembling, but there was nothing tentative about the way she was looking at him. "Yes. I am."

If he'd been hot for her a few minutes ago, he was past

the boiling point now. Although he was shaking, he managed to cradle her in his arms and roll her on top of him without either of them landing on the floor.

Her eager gaze swept over him. Then she reached behind her and picked up the red pillow they'd tossed to the end of the sofa to make room for their writhing bodies. "Lift up your head," she directed in a husky voice.

Moments later she reversed her position over his quaking body. Her mouth slid over his penis as he began to pleasure her with his tongue, causing her to quiver and moan above him. As far as he was concerned, this could last forever.

But her hunger for him guaranteed otherwise. That and the sweet nectar on his tongue made him pulse with need and draw closer...and closer yet. He felt his control going even as he knew that he needed a few more seconds to bring her to the edge. A few more...and then he came, shuddering and groaning as he pressed his mouth deeper.

He felt the first quake run through her. He moved his tongue faster. Warm breath tickled his penis as she took her mouth away and began to whimper. Another quake, and another.

He was crazy about this woman. Crazy in love with her. Pressing the tips of his fingers into her smooth bottom he pulled her in even tighter, and that's when he sent her over. Joy rolled through him as he lay with his head between her thighs and listened to her cries.

What a great start to the evening.

THE THING ABOUT MAKING LOVE in the middle of the living room, Suzanne discovered, was that there were no covers to pull up afterward. She and Greg had rearranged themselves so that they were curled in each other's arms, but an afghan would have helped keep her from feeling quite so exposed.

Greg didn't seem bothered at all. He smoothed her hair and kissed her. "That was amazing. You are amazing."

"You, too," she said.

He looked into her eyes. "And?"

This guy didn't miss a trick, she thought. "And now I feel really naked lying here on the sofa."

He chuckled. "Not a problem. Rome wasn't built in a day."

"You mean that eventually I'll become a nudist?"

His chuckle became a laugh. "I don't know. Maybe. That's never interested me, but if it intrigues you, then—"

"It doesn't! I can't imagine walking around outdoors with no clothes on."

He gave her a quick kiss. "I can imagine that. I just wouldn't want anybody to be there except you. Now come on, let's get dressed. I want to take you where there are people, and for that we need clothes."

"Okay." She stood and quickly gathered her clothes from the floor. Taking them off in the living room hadn't seemed nearly so intimate as putting them on with Greg watching. "If you don't mind, I'll dress in my bedroom. I might take a quick shower, too."

"If you want." He looked amused. "Want me to go back to my apartment and take one? Sort of start over?"

She backed toward the bedroom, holding her clothes in front of her. "That seems kind of silly. I'm sure you're fine. I just…"

"Go ahead." Already wearing his navy briefs, he'd plopped down on the sofa to put on his socks. "Do whatever you like to feel comfortable. When you're finished, I'll come in and comb my hair."

She appreciated his sensitivity in giving her some space.

"Thanks, Greg. I suppose I'm not making sense. After what we just...did...you're probably wondering why I'm suddenly feeling—"

"I'm not wondering that at all." He fixed a warm gaze on her. "You don't have to tell me that you stepped out of your comfort zone just now. I'm forever grateful that you did, but I can understand if that makes you a little nervous. Take your time."

What an incredible guy. She had the urge to run over and kiss him, but doing that while she was clutching an armload of clothes over her nakedness wouldn't be the smoothest maneuver she'd ever tried. "Thanks." She smiled at him. "I won't be long."

As a compromise, she left her bedroom door open. She even left the bathroom door open as she walked in with her clothes pressed against her body. Then she caught sight of herself looking like a virgin who had been ravished within an inch of her life, and she had to grin at her modesty, all things considered.

First she'd propositioned the guy and then suggested something pretty radical—for her, at least. She'd liked it, too. Liked it a lot. After such a wild adventure, she ought to be ready to parade around naked in front of Greg without a second thought. But she wasn't. Maybe with his accepting attitude she might eventually feel free enough to do that, but not yet.

Shaking out her clothes, she lay them over the vanity, grabbed a scrunchie from the drawer under the sink and pulled her tousled hair back before turning on the shower. She didn't spend much time under the spray, but she was aware as she ran a soapy washcloth quickly over her body that she'd never felt so alive. Yes, her thighs were still sore from her gym session, but she'd forgotten all about that in the heat of the moment.

Greg's loving was part of the reason that she felt so vibrant, but she suspected there was more going on than that. Taking the initiative as she had with this relationship had given her the sort of adrenaline rush that she imagined skydivers experienced when they leaped from a plane. She was beginning to like taking risks.

Or maybe she liked taking them with Greg, she thought as she toweled off and rubbed lotion on her body. Craving Greg on a regular basis could be dangerous, but his all-out style of loving and his tenderness afterward didn't inspire her to caution. No matter how often she told herself that he would walk away soon, she had a hard time believing it. He acted like a guy who was becoming involved with her. Very involved.

Maybe he had that effect on all the women he slept with, and was totally unaware that he gave the impression that he was falling in love. Even casual comments led her to believe it, like when he mentioned that he couldn't imagine walking around naked outdoors unless she happened to be the only person there. That sounded like a man who was starting to think in exclusive terms.

Or maybe he was loose with words. As she pulled on her clothes, she reminded herself that this affair had begun because she'd gone down to his apartment and asked him for exactly that. All he was doing was satisfying her request.

Yet she hadn't asked him to take her out tonight. She was puzzled that he'd decided to do that after she'd warned him that she might be going overboard emotionally. She'd given him the perfect out with her little good-bye speech, and he hadn't taken it.

Thank goodness he hadn't. She hated to think that she'd almost missed out on one of the most exciting lovemaking episodes of her life. She quickly reapplied her makeup and brushed her hair until it shone. Everything was back together except for putting on her snow boots, which she'd left out in the living room.

With a sense of anticipation, she walked into the living room, only to find it empty. "Greg?"

"In here." His voice came from the kitchen.

Padding into the kitchen in her socks, she found him using a small screwdriver attached to his key ring to tighten her paper-towel holder. In the midst of all the excitement, he hadn't forgotten that it had been loose the other night when he'd been here.

"Ready?" he asked, his back to her as he twisted the screw a couple of times more.

"Uh-huh." She gazed at the pattern his hair made as it swirled to a vee at his nape. She admired the broad expanse of his shoulders under the green plaid shirt and the sexy angle of his hips as he leaned against the counter. She was ready, all right—ready to make love to him again.

But she was also ready for more than that. She'd always imagined that her future husband would turn out to be somebody like Jared, someone in the financial world who worked downtown and lived the same kind of high-stress life that she did. She knew couples like that, two people who kept track of each other through pagers and cell phones. They seemed happy with the pace, maybe even thrived on it.

"I'll be done in a sec. This other one's loose, too." Greg shifted the small screwdriver to the other end of the bracket.

As she watched him work, she thought of how soothing it would be to come home at the end of a frantic day and find a man like Greg waiting for her. Because he wasn't caught up in the rat race, he could provide a refuge from it. Her throat tightened with longing.

According to Terri, Greg wasn't interested in settling

down. Terri was convinced that he'd created the perfect bachelor existence in this apartment building full of needy women, and would probably laugh if anybody suggested he change his circumstances. Suzanne kept trying to fit the Greg she knew into that picture, but she wasn't having any luck. He didn't act like a Casanova. He acted like a forever kind of guy.

"That does it." He turned and his gaze swept over her. "You look great. I really do love that sweater."

She glanced down at the bright patterns woven into the wool. Then she decided to take a risk. "I guess this would be the right thing to wear if you were spending the weekend at a cottage in Wisconsin," she said.

He didn't blink and grow pale, as a cornered Casanova might. Instead, he met her gaze. "Exactly," he said.

Warmth traveled through her. Either she was a lousy judge of people, or Greg was really and truly interested.

"And now we need to get out of here." He took her by the arm and steered her toward the living room. "Otherwise, I'm liable to take that great-looking sweater off you again, and we might never leave."

TWO HOURS LATER, Greg was having a terrific time, and his heart was brimming with hope that his instincts about Suzanne hadn't been wrong. Even the bus ride over to Jerry's had been fun. They'd found a seat in the back and snuggled like a couple of love-struck high-school kids while they looked out at the Christmas lights along the way.

Jerry's was crowded with the darts tournament regulars, and the little pub seemed even cozier than normal with all its Christmas decorations. His friends had greeted Suzanne with warmth and carefully controlled curiosity. They might well be curious since he'd never brought a date here. Even Rachel, bless her heart, had been nice to Suzanne.

Suzanne had responded exactly the way he'd hoped she would. If the bad grammar and unsophisticated conversation bothered her, she gave no indication. She ate hot dogs and drank beer with obvious enjoyment. At one point she'd ended up with a cute little foam mustache and he'd barely kept himself from kissing it away. Then he'd watched with rapt attention and growing arousal while she licked it off.

Now the darts tournament was in full swing, and Suzanne was guaranteed to come in dead last. She didn't seem to care. Laughing, she heaved another dart at the board and completely missed the target. His friends were really razzing her, too, pretending to crawl under the tables when it was her turn so they'd be safe.

"You like her a lot, huh?" Rachel said softly, coming up next to him with a mug of beer in her hand.

Greg glanced into Rachel's brown eyes and saw no animosity there. She was a class act. "Yeah, I do. But you know, I'm sorry that—"

She laid a finger against his mouth. "Never mind." She stroked his cheek. "I had my doubts all along, but I tried to force it because you're such a great catch."

"I'm not so sure about that."

"I am. And so is she. You make a cute couple. Invite me to the wedding." With a smile, Rachel left before Greg could protest that he and Suzanne were miles away from getting married.

Of course they were. Miles away. And yet every time he looked at Suzanne he became more convinced that he wanted to share his life with her. She seemed to be moving in that same direction.

He'd been encouraged by the delight in her eyes when

she found him fixing her paper-towel rack. Unless he missed his guess, she'd enjoyed having him perform that little domestic chore. Maybe she was beginning to think that she didn't want a guy who went to work wearing a suit and tie. Maybe she fancied herself hooked up with a handyman.

But they needed to have a conversation about his job situation before he focused too intently on the sound of wedding bells. She still could be planning to remodel him into the man she thought he could be. In his experience, women couldn't seem to resist that urge.

"Greg!" Murph, one of his buddies who drove a delivery truck, called over to him. "You're up, champ. Let's see if you've still got it."

As it turned out, his aim was off tonight. He should have known it would be. Instead of concentrating on the dart game, he was thinking about impressing Suzanne. She seemed to be impressed anyway, which felt damn good.

He'd been eager to bring her here, but now that he could see that she fit right in, he was just as eager to get her back to the apartment. They had some talking to do. Among other things. Imagining those other things, he threw a dart into the wall, missing the target even worse than she had.

Later, as they were finally saying their goodbyes and heading out of the pub, Murph grabbed a moment when Suzanne was talking to one of the other women. Throwing an arm around Greg's shoulders, he took him aside.

"She's hell on your dart game, but I like her," Murph said. "This one's a keeper."

"I'm glad you think so," Greg said carefully. "But we're just friends."

"Rachel doesn't think so," Murph said. "And neither do I. Oh, and just so you know, since you seem to have backed off with Rach, I'm moving in."

"That's terrific." Greg smiled at his friend. "She's a wonderful woman. We just didn't have the right combination. I hope it works out for you two."

"I have a feeling it might. We've been friends for years. Thought we'd try getting a little more friendly." He glanced toward the door. "I think your lady is ready to go. Seriously, I'd try to hang on to this one. She suits you. She's smart, like you."

Greg tried to brush that remark aside, but Murph held up one big hand. "Listen, everybody knows you're some sort of brainiac. We all kind of like it. Keeps us on our toes. Now take off, before she finds somebody she likes better and leaves with him, instead."

Outside, snow was coming down and the wind had picked up. Greg glanced at Suzanne. "Let's go back inside and I'll call a cab."

"Oh, don't be silly." She grabbed his arm and tugged in the direction of the bus stop about a half block away. "The bus is fine."

He resisted. "I can afford a cab, Suzanne."

She stopped and gazed up at him. She'd pulled up the hood on her wool coat and she looked adorable. "I know you can," she said, her breath making clouds in the air. "But I'll tell you a secret. Cabs remind me of the kind of dates I used to have, where we'd go to the trendiest restaurants and eat whatever ethnic food was in that week, and then take another cab to some hot nightspot so that we could see and be seen by the right people."

He forgot the wind and the snow and the cold. Nothing mattered but the look in her eyes as she told him exactly what he wanted to hear. "You won't get a night like that out of me."

"I know, and that's what makes you so special."

He pulled her into his arms and kissed her, kissed her so

thoroughly that her hood fell back. Their kiss was so hot that he wouldn't have been surprised to see that they'd melted the ice on the sidewalk where they were standing. No telling how long he might have kept it up, but he heard the airbrake release on the city bus.

Breaking the kiss, he grabbed Suzanne's hand and yelled at the bus driver as he started to run. The driver waited, and they boarded a nearly empty bus.

"You two might want to move to the back seat," the driver said, glancing at them with amusement as he closed the doors with a slap of rubber molding.

Greg recognized him. Stan was a regular on this run. "Thanks for waiting."

"Not a problem." He grinned. "After all, it's Christmas."

It sure did feel like Christmas, Greg thought as he kept a steadying hand on Suzanne's shoulder during their lurching progress to the back of the moving bus. Christmas hadn't felt this special since the year he'd turned nine and Santa had brought him a silver and black motocross bike.

At last he and Suzanne settled into the seat and he pulled her close. "Cold?"

She snuggled against him and turned her face up to his. Her cheeks were bright pink from the wind. "How could I be with a guy like you around?"

"Glad to be of service."

She gazed at him. "Now that we're alone, will you tell me about Rachel?"

His heart leaped with happiness at the knowledge that his dealings with other women mattered to her. If she had no stake in their relationship, other women wouldn't matter a bit. "Sure," he said. "I'll tell you about Rachel. What do you want to know?"

13

WHAT SUZANNE REALLY wanted to know was how many women Greg had been involved with recently. The apartment-building ladies alone should have kept him plenty busy, judging from the way Terri had explained things. Now Suzanne had met another woman who felt comfortable touching Greg's mouth and stroking his cheek, signals that Suzanne took to mean they'd been intimate. Suzanne was beginning to think she'd been lucky to find a vacant spot in Greg's packed schedule.

"Rachel's a wonderful person." Greg combed his fingers through Suzanne's windblown hair as he talked.

She had to suppress her jealousy. She didn't want to hear that, even if she suspected it was true. "I can see she is."

"We were both involved in the darts tournament every week, and we became friends," Greg continued. "About six months ago, we made the mistake of taking it beyond that, and we both knew pretty quickly that we shouldn't have."

Suzanne wasn't sure that Rachel had known all that quickly. Rachel still seemed quite fond of Greg. Way too fond. "You don't have to answer this if you don't want to," she said, aware that she might be invading his personal space. "But she seemed very nice, and I think she still likes you...a lot. So why wouldn't it work?"

"It's my fault." Greg settled a little farther back in the

seat, bringing Suzanne with him. Then he leaned over and kissed her on the forehead before settling his cheek on the top of her head. "Rachel's great, but after we finished...well, after all was said and done, we had nothing to talk about."

"Oh." She didn't like having him confirm, however subtly, that he'd slept with Rachel, but even more amazing was his reason for discontinuing that activity. It was the exact reason Terri had given for why Suzanne wouldn't want a permanent relationship with Greg. How ironic.

"I found out that being able to talk to a woman is actually more important to me than...other things."

Suzanne gave a little murmur of agreement. Well, that certainly explained his activities in the apartment building, where he could find a slew of good conversationalists. How strange that none of them had been able to see past his job and realize that he was as intelligent and well read as they were.

"Any more questions?" he asked.

She had dozens of questions, but she was afraid to ask them. She wondered if he'd taken any of the other women at the apartment to Jerry's for hot dogs, beer and darts. She wondered if her time with him had a limit, and how she'd know when they'd reached it. And most of all, she wondered if this love affair was different, more special, than the many others he'd had.

It certainly was special for her, but she didn't have his vast experience. Maybe this heady excitement and daring sense of adventure were commonplace for him. And maybe the cozy security she felt in his arms, a sense of belonging that she'd never known before with any man, was an illusion.

"You're being awfully quiet," Greg said. "Are you sure you don't have any more questions?"

Taking a deep breath, she tried to work up the courage to say what was on her mind. But if she broached the subject and discovered that she was as temporary a lover as all the others had been, then she'd have to end their relationship tonight. She couldn't make love to him again knowing that she would be replaced soon.

She'd already allowed her heart to become too involved as it was. Come to think of it, if he planned to end their affair she'd probably have to move to another apartment building. Living where he did and knowing he was taking some other tenant to bed would be torture beyond endurance.

"I know something's bothering you," he said. "Let me guess what it is."

No, she didn't want to have this conversation now. She was selfish enough to yearn for one more glorious night of lovemaking before they talked about this. "Nothing's bothering me." She shifted her position in order to look into his eyes as she laid her hand on his thigh. "Except that this bus ride seems longer going home than it did getting there."

Desire flared in his eyes. "True." He closed his hand over hers and squeezed it against his thigh. "But before we finish this very long bus ride, I think we need to get something out in the open."

"No, we don't." She tried to move her hand higher.

His grip tightened. "Yes, we do. Don't you want to know—"

"Nope. Don't ask, don't tell. That's my philosophy."

"Come on, Suzanne. You have to be curious as to why I'm a janitor."

"What?"

"You've seen all the books, and I even admitted reading most of them. You have to be wondering why I don't finish college at the least, or go out and get a better paying, more prestigious job at the most."

She stared at him. Of all the things she was curious about, that was at the bottom of the list. In fact, one of his most appealing qualities was his lack of pretension. If he found satisfaction in his job, which left him the leisure to explore all kinds of subjects on his own, she thought that was fine.

"Did I guess?" he asked quietly.

"No." But she'd seen the change in his expression. This was a loaded subject for him, apparently. "No, you didn't even come close," she said. "But I have a strong feeling that somebody you cared about disapproved of your choices. So that's the question I'd like to ask. Who was she?"

At first he looked too shocked to reply. Then a distinct wariness appeared in his green eyes. His guard was definitely up.

"Okay. You don't have to tell me." Of the various secrets he was keeping—his cat, his extensive library and his extracurricular activities with the female tenants—this might be the biggest one, the one he was least likely to part with and the most critical to figuring him out. But she wasn't about to force it out of him.

"You don't have to tell me anything, Greg," she added. "But I want you to know that how you've chosen to make your living is not a problem for me. Not even slightly."

"You're absolutely sure about that?" He still didn't seem inclined to believe it.

"Absolutely." Then she snuggled against him again. "Your place or mine?"

"Mine." Greg wasn't about to mess up what promised to be a wonderful end to the evening by demanding they get into a big discussion. He lowered his voice. "I'm the only one with condoms," he reminded her.

"Oh, right."

Greg was happy that they'd settled the issue of his employment so easily. Or rather, he ought to be happy. Mostly he was confused. He'd expected at least some hassle from Suzanne about his handyman job. At the very least, he'd thought she'd want him to explain his reasoning for staying with it. But never in his wildest dreams had he imagined that she'd accept his job without question.

The bus driver automatically pulled over at the stop nearest Greg and Suzanne's apartment building. Stan had been bringing Greg home from Jerry's for the better part of a year, and he didn't need a signal from Greg.

"Let's go," Greg said softly, hugging Suzanne close as they stood and prepared to exit from the rear doors. "Thanks, Stan," he called up to the front. "Happy holidays."

"Same to you," Stan called back.

Wind and snow swirled around them as they stepped down to the sidewalk. Greg made sure Suzanne's hood was up, and he kept his arm around her shoulders as they hurried toward the apartment-house entrance. It was too cold and windy to make small talk.

Between the late hour and the weather, he didn't expect anybody to be hanging around the lobby and notice them together. He'd been a little worried about that on the way out, but they hadn't met anyone in the elevator or the lobby. Of course they'd walked out nonchalantly, not even holding hands, so their being together could have seemed like an accident.

But with her tucked inside his arm this way, nobody would believe they'd met by accident. They were obviously coming in from a date. He wasn't quite sure what might happen if somebody did see them. Perhaps nothing. Or perhaps a tenant would start gossiping and word would get back to his employers.

At this point he didn't much care. If Suzanne truly accepted his lifestyle, there was a good chance that his place of employment was about to change anyway. If they became a couple, they'd probably choose a different place to live, which would mean he'd have to find another handyman position.

Or maybe they wouldn't become a couple, after all. He could think of two reasons why Suzanne didn't care what he did for a living. Either she was the kind of person who believed in letting people do whatever made them happy, or this relationship wasn't important enough for her to worry about the type of job he had.

An optimist would go for the first scenario, a pessimist the second. When he was a younger man he'd been an incurable optimist, but Amelia had taken a big chunk of that optimism with her when she'd left. He knew what he wanted to believe about Suzanne, but he wasn't sure that he could.

They arrived at the apartment's front entrance, and he used his key to get them in. They bustled into the lobby, stomping snow from their boots.

Suzanne threw back her hood and pulled off her gloves. Her teeth were chattering. "The w-wind must be coming off the l-lake."

"Must be." He could hardly wait to get her someplace where he could help her warm up. Really warm up. "Do you need to go up to your apartment for anything?"

"Nope." Her eyes glowed with barely contained excitement.

"Good. Then let's take the stairs down. It's faster, and besides—"

The lobby doors opened again, bringing in a rush of snowy air and a burst of female chatter. Greg turned, figuring there was no way he and Suzanne would be able to sneak down those stairs now. Might as well brave it out. Just his luck, Jennifer and Carolyn, two of the women he'd counseled about their love lives, were standing there looking extremely curious.

Maybe this was a good thing. He'd let Suzanne decide how to handle this. If she wanted to be open about their relationship, so much the better. In fact, he'd take that as a very good sign, if she was willing to go public with the news that they were seeing each other.

Suzanne remained silent.

"Hi, Jennifer, Carolyn," Greg said, to break the tension. "Pretty cold out there, huh?"

"Sure is." Jennifer spoke and bobbed her head in agreement, but Carolyn appeared to be struck speechless.

"We, um, went to a concert," Jennifer added.

Beside him, Suzanne cleared her throat. Here it came. If she implied that they'd had an honest-to-goodness date, then he could believe she was in this relationship for real.

"Greg was telling me about this darts tournament he plays in every week," she said. "I love darts, so he took me over there so I could get into it."

Disappointment knifed through him. "Yeah, and she kicked butt, too." He turned to her. "Well, see you around, Suzanne."

"See you, Greg."

Her eyes were trying to tell him something, but he wasn't sure what. And maybe it didn't matter. Maybe this was how it would end. Pasting a smile on his face, he turned away and walked toward the door that opened onto the building's stairwell. Maybe, once she was safely inside her apartment, she'd call him. Or maybe she would never call him again.

SUZANNE'S HEART WRENCHED as Greg walked away. She had the feeling she'd said the wrong thing, but she'd only been trying to protect his job. Besides, the situation had been extremely awkward, standing there with Jennifer and Carolyn. Carolyn was probably another of Greg's "projects," judging from the way she'd been struck dumb by seeing Suzanne obviously coming in from some type of evening activity with Greg.

Suzanne's first thought had been that he'd want her to minimize what they'd shared, considering he was facing two of his former lovers. Yet he hadn't seemed very happy about her comment. Or maybe she was reading too much into the way he'd reacted.

"Well, I'm ready to head upstairs," Jennifer said. "I have to get up early and do some Christmas shopping."

"I'm not done, either," Suzanne said, heading for the elevator. For one thing, she had to decide whether a gift for Greg was appropriate. She wanted to get him something, but if she gave him a present and he didn't reciprocate, that could be a clumsy moment.

Carolyn, a petite redhead, spoke for the first time as the three women walked toward the elevator. "So you and Greg are spending some time together?"

Suzanne punched the elevator button before turning toward Carolyn. "Sort of."

Carolyn gazed at her with obvious envy in her eyes. "I didn't know he played darts."

"I didn't, either," Jennifer said. "I'll bet that was fun."

"It was okay." Suzanne wanted nothing more than to get away from these two. Being with them only reminded her of the carefree love life Greg had indulged in before now and that might continue once she was old news.

"He's a great guy," Carolyn said. "Terrific listener."

"Isn't he, though?" Jennifer agreed. "You feel as if you could tell that man simply *anything*."

But he didn't tell them much at all, Suzanne thought. He had a whole other life full of friends and family, and she'd bet these two women knew nothing more about Greg than his abilities in bed. Unfortunately, that was more knowledge than Suzanne thought either of them should have.

If they didn't care enough about the guy to find out who he was, then they didn't deserve what he had to offer. Terri might think Greg was living in some kind of bachelor paradise, but Suzanne saw it differently. These women were taking advantage of him, using him to make themselves feel better and giving very little back.

"Don't you agree, Suzanne?" Jennifer asked. "Isn't Greg just so easy to talk to?"

"Yeah," she said. "Greg's the best." Mercifully, at that moment the elevator arrived at hers and Jennifer's floor. "Gotta run," she said to Jennifer, to forestall any more conversation. "I drank too many beers at the pub, if you know what I mean." She dashed to her door, opened it and escaped inside.

Once there, she threw off her coat and walked over to the phone. But once the receiver was in her hand, she began to rethink calling him. No, she needed to look into his eyes while she explained herself. He needed to know that she wasn't just using him for sex, like all the other women in this building. And maybe, just maybe, she'd find the courage to tell him how much she cared.

"MATILDA, I guess I struck out again." Greg had calculated how much time it would take Suzanne to ride the elevator to her apartment, pick up the phone and call him. Even allowing for some obligatory conversation with Jennifer and Carolyn, she'd had more than enough time by now. Apparently she wasn't going to call.

He wandered into the bedroom, his socks whispering on the carpet. Earlier today he'd put new votives in the candleholders and fresh sheets on the bed. He'd even made a quick trip to the florist to pick up a single red rose and a bud vase to put it in.

Matilda followed him into the bedroom.

"I hope you like the rose, Matilda. Looks like you're going to be the only female here to appreciate it." He reached down and picked her up, taking comfort in her reassuring warmth and the steady rumble of her purr as he cradled her in his arms.

She kneaded her claws against his shoulder.

"I thought I had a shot this time, kitty-cat," he said, looking into her yellow eyes. "It could be my fault for not telling Suzanne about Amelia when I had the chance. Or maybe nothing would have made a difference." He leaned down and rubbed his cheek against Matilda's soft fur, his throat tight with disappointment. "At any rate, it looks like she's gone."

The doorbell buzzed and Matilda launched herself from his arms, digging through the flannel shirt in her startled haste. He hardly noticed the prick of pain from her claws. He could only imagine one person who would be ringing his doorbell at this hour of the night.

Heart racing, he walked to the door and opened it to find Suzanne standing there wearing her long wool coat and snow boots. The coat was unbuttoned, but she was holding it together as if she felt cold. It was chilly in the basement, but not that chilly. He couldn't imagine why she hadn't left her coat and boots upstairs, unless they were part of her plan to confuse people.

He was certainly confused. "Are we going somewhere?" he asked.

"I hope not. I was feeling a little stiff, and I wondered if you knew where I could get a good massage." With a smile, she opened the coat.

He'd visited the Art Institute of Chicago, had seen some classical nudes there, statues that were supposed to represent the ideal woman. Not a single one compared with the sight of Suzanne's rosy, naked body. His chest tightened with admiration. And gratitude. He was so thankful that she was really here, offering herself to him.

Maybe she hadn't been willing to acknowledge him as her date in front of the other women. Maybe she would spend only a few more fantastic nights with him and call it quits. He didn't care. He'd take what he could get.

He cleared the huskiness from his throat. "I might be able to take care of that massage request, if you'd like to step inside."

"I would."

He moved back to let her walk in. "I'm not a professional, but my price is reasonable."

"That's good to know."

By the time he'd closed the door, locked it and turned around to face her, she'd stepped out of her boots and discarded her coat.

His throat closed with longing. She was so damn beautiful, and now at last she knew it. She stood in the middle of his living room wearing nothing but a smile. Not a trace of embarrassment lingered in her blue eyes. Instead, she looked provocative and...proud. Yes, that was the emotion that shone in those eyes, one he hadn't seen there before. She was proud of this gift she had brought him.

"You're magnificent," he murmured.

"Thank you." Her gaze flickered downward, to where she's dropped her coat.

Matilda was sniffing it with great interest. Then she turned around twice and curled up in its folds.

"I think your cat prefers my coat to me," she said.

"Silly cat." Greg held out his hand. "Come with me, fair lady." Working hard to breathe normally, he led her toward the bedroom, where he'd left the bedside lamp burning instead of the candles. "Candlelight? Or do you want—"

"The lamp is perfect." Releasing his hand, she threw back the covers and stretched out on the sheets. "So we can see each other."

He quivered with anticipation as he unbuttoned his shirt. "Yes."

Her gaze grew serious. "Greg, I was only trying to protect your job back there in the lobby."

"I don't care about the job," he said gently.

"You don't? But I thought—"

"You know what? It doesn't matter." He was prepared to live in the present. For now, she was here, waiting for him to love her.

"I just...well, it seemed as if what I said bothered you."

"What is said or done outside this room isn't important." He tossed aside his jeans and socks and left on his briefs. Whether she knew it or not, she really was going to get a massage. First.

"It is important if it makes you feel used."

He smiled at that. "Used for what?"

"You know. For...for sex."

He thought of all they'd shared in the past few days. "I don't feel used, Suzanne. I feel privileged."

She gazed at him for a long time, and a sheen of moisture

sparkled in her eyes. She swallowed. "You always know exactly what to say."

Except when it counted, like during the bus ride when she'd wanted him to open up about Amelia and he hadn't been able to step over the barriers he'd been erecting for years. "I don't always know," he murmured. "Now close your eyes, pretty lady." He picked up the bottle of massage oil. "I'm going to make you feel good all over."

14

SUZANNE CLOSED HER EYES and abandoned herself to Greg with a kind of surrender she'd never allowed herself with any man. When he lifted her and positioned her closer to the end of the bed, she went limp in his arms, as if she were a rag doll.

The mattress moved under his weight, and she was vaguely aware that he'd moved the pillows out of the way so he could kneel at her head. Then the scent of almonds swirled around her as he stroked her forehead, her cheeks and the line of her jaw.

"Let go, Suzanne." He circled his fingers lightly over her mouth until all the tiny muscles loosened and her lips parted. "Like that." Cupping her chin, he slid both hands slowly toward her ears and paused there to massage the lobes.

Then he cradled her head in his hands. "Relax your neck. Let me hold you," he whispered.

She did, and it was the most incredible feeling to lie with her head resting there, supported by his strong fingers. Trust flowed between them in smooth, unbroken waves, and she sighed with pleasure.

His voice was soft, almost as if he were speaking from inside her mind. "They say that making love can be...spiritual."

"Mmm." She believed Greg could take her to that place where making love would be like that.

"I always wondered what they meant." He leaned over her, brushing her lips with his as he tucked a pillow under her head. "I think we're going to find out."

She thought so, too. She felt liquid and heavy with promise, like a dark, rich plum ready to be plucked. Yearning to be plucked...and savored.

Beneath Greg's oiled hands, her shoulders lost all rigidity as she seemed to sink deeper into the mattress. Then he shifted again, and she opened her eyes to find him astride her, sitting back on his heels, careful not to rest his weight on her. He picked up her hand and began a slow massage of each finger.

Her gaze drifted to his briefs, where his erection jutted beneath the navy cotton. Then she looked into his eyes again.

His mouth curved in response to her unspoken question. "I'm afraid your masseur has trouble maintaining his cool."

Her vocal cords felt rusty, but she managed a single word. "Good."

"Now just close your eyes," he said gently.

She obeyed, so mesmerized by his sensual touch that she wouldn't dream of resisting. As he kneaded the muscles in her arms, his clever hands found erogenous zones no one had ever discovered. Or perhaps she was ultrasensitive, her body charged with the knowledge that she'd given him permission to stroke every inch of her with those almond-scented fingertips.

She felt the blood racing through her veins and her nerves tingling in reaction. Yet even so, she grew more languid and incapable of movement. Like ripening fruit, she waited for the moment when he would nudge the branch and she would fall, juicy and warm, into his outstretched hands.

A drop of oil landed softly on her breast and rolled slowly toward her cleavage. Another drop followed, and another. Moisture pooled in her mouth. Oil dripped on her other breast, followed by the click of the bottle being set back on the nightstand. Anticipation curled in her stomach.

With firm strokes he spread the oil over her breasts—creating ever-tighter circles, closing in on her taut nipples. At last he stroked upward, as if creating those quivering peaks, squeezing and coaxing them into tight buds. She had become his work of art.

His touch remained steady and rhythmic, but his breathing had changed, becoming rougher, louder. She smiled, knowing that he'd caught himself in his own net.

"That's right," he murmured. "I can't turn you on without turning myself on, too."

"Do you..." She paused and ran her tongue over her lips. "Do you want to...make love to me...now?"

"I am making love to you." There was amusement in his voice.

"I mean—"

"I know. Not yet."

Unconsciously she arched upward. "Are you sure?"

"Yes." He pressed on her shoulders, guiding her back to the mattress. "Lie still."

"I don't know if I can."

"Try. Try to stay relaxed, no matter how I touch you. Pretend that you're a warm piece of clay."

"I feel...more like a lava flow."

"You feel like an angel." He stroked her rib cage. "With a bit of devil in her."

She loved his hands there, but she wanted them lower. Her body remembered the delight those hands could bring, and the yearning had begun from the moment he'd touched her. As he dropped more oil on her belly, she moaned, wanting him to slip between her thighs, part her curls and use those knowing hands to shower her with ecstasy.

Instead, he circled her stomach and stroked down over her hipbones, arching away from the spot that pulsed with longing.

She moved restlessly beneath him. "Greg..."

"I will," he murmured. "Lie still."

She was on fire for him. Containing that fire, forcing herself to lie quietly while he moved to her feet and massaged each toe, was torture, but so sweet, so erotic, that she imagined even her cells had begun to vibrate in anticipation. No matter where he touched her—the arch of her foot, the curve of her ankle, the back of her knee—she felt that touch in the throbbing center of her femininity.

He dripped more oil on her inner thighs and began to knead the muscles there. They were still sore from her workout, but the slight pain mattered so little compared to the tactile pleasure of his hands moving over her body.

And then...at long last, he spread her legs. The dribble of oil over her damp curls felt cool, like the slide of chocolate syrup over her heat. She trembled.

"Easy." His voice rasped with eagerness. "Stay still." He stroked her gently, using both hands, keeping to the outer folds.

She began to pant, the sound of her breathing mingling with his harsh gasps. When he parted her and stroked deeper, she started to lift her hips. With steady pressure, he urged her back down, holding her still with one hand while he massaged her more deeply.

Her climax happened in a rush, coursing through her in a tidal wave of sensation, blotting out everything but the tremors that spread in pulsing waves, consuming her. She lost all sense of time and place, barely registered that he was no longer touching her, that he'd left the bed. Still the tremors continued.

She was still shaking when he moved over her and with one thrust of his hips, slipped deep inside. Then he settled gently against her oiled body, giving her just enough of his weight that his chest hair lightly grazed her breasts.

"Open your eyes," he said hoarsely.

Her lids were so heavy. She lifted them with effort and struggled to focus. At last she could see him—his green eyes lit with passion and something more. There was far more than lust in the way he was looking at her. Her heart surged with joy.

"People can make love for years and never really know each other," he murmured, his voice unsteady. "But I know you, Suzanne." He anchored himself even tighter. "I know you."

"Yes." Her body continued to quiver as she reached up and cupped his face. "Yes."

"And when I'm inside you like this, it's as if I know...everything of importance in the world."

She nodded, too filled with emotion to speak. She'd never felt this close to anyone. In her limited experience, making love had been...nice. She'd had no idea that a climax could shatter her this way.

His voice was hoarse with emotion. "I almost hate to move. This is so perfect."

"I know." No matter what happened, she would never forget this moment as he lay with her, his body covering hers, blended with hers, touching the intimate core of her.

"But I...I need..." He eased back and closed his eyes before pushing home again. *"That."* When he opened his eyes, the blaze was out of control and his breath came in harsh gasps.

With only that easy friction, he'd set her on fire. She slipped her hands down to his hips and pressed her fingers into his tight bottom. "So do I."

With a groan, he began to move within her.

As sensations bombarded her, she struggled for breath. "Good," she whispered.

"More than good." He thrust faster. "This is...paradise. Ah...that's it. Move with me, Suzanne."

She rose to meet his thrusts because she couldn't do otherwise. Her body quaked with each penetration, and her smile trembled as she gazed up at him. "You don't want me...to lie still...anymore?"

"No." His answering smile was tight with tension. "Go wild." He gasped and pumped faster. "Scratch and claw if you want."

She did want that. He was driving her out of her mind, and her fingernails raked his bottom, urging him on.

She clutched at him, her body writhing and hot, demanding the orgasm that he promised with each thrust. When at last she reached it, she arched upward with a moan of triumph.

He drove once more into her quivering body and came, shuddering against her as he uttered a low, keening cry of release.

As that vulnerable cry echoed in the small room, as she held him close while they rode the aftershocks, she fell completely, irrevocably in love.

"HER NAME WAS AMELIA," Greg murmured as they lay together in the early-morning hours. They'd made love twice more, and he knew that soon she'd have to sneak back upstairs. After all, she'd come down wearing only her coat and boots. He could understand why she wouldn't want to be caught in the hall like that. But before she left, he needed to tell her about Amelia.

All traces of sleepiness left Suzanne's gaze. "The woman who didn't think you should aspire to be a handyman?" she said.

"A girl more than a woman." He pulled the covers over her bare shoulder, not wanting her to get chilled. "We met in college."

"So you went to college?"

Six hours ago her surprised question might have put him on the defensive, but he knew Suzanne now. She wasn't a snob, and there was no hidden agenda in her question. "I'd always planned to go, so I saved from the time I could earn my own money. I figured that was the only way I'd get there, because my grades weren't going to earn me any scholarships."

"Now, *that* surprises me." She traced the line of his jaw with one finger. "You're obviously a scholar, so why wouldn't you get good grades?"

He shrugged. "I never liked the regimentation of high school. I had higher hopes for college, but to be honest, I was having trouble with the assembly-line atmosphere there, too. I loved the subjects but I hated the way they were taught, at least to the underclassmen. Everybody said upper-level classes were better, so I was holding out for those. But then my dad died, and I decided to drop out."

She looked confused. "Because…?"

This was the part that always made him uncomfortable. "I don't want you to think I'm some sort of martyr, because I'm not. But my dad never bothered with life insurance, so my mom was strapped. I gave her the money I'd saved for college."

"Oh, Greg, that's so sad."

"It's not sad. At the time I felt like it was a huge sacrifice, and unfortunately I'm afraid my mom still thinks so. But I didn't belong in college. I've been far happier studying all this stuff on my own. And if I'd gotten a degree, I would have felt honor-bound to use it in some profession." He realized what a relief it was to finally talk to someone who would understand. "I like being a handyman."

Suzanne gazed at him. "You know, sometimes when people are forced into making choices like that, they justify it as being for the best, when it really—"

"I'm telling you, it was for the best." He heard the sharpness in his voice, and realized he might not completely trust her with this, after all.

"You didn't let me finish," she said, her voice calm. "I was going to say, but in this case, I believe you. I think it was for the best."

"Oh." He let out a breath. "Most people don't react that way."

"I'm sure." She stroked his hair. "But I'm not most people."

He caught her hand and brought it to his lips. "No, you most certainly aren't," he said, kissing each finger in turn.

"I'm not Amelia, for example."

"No." He brushed her knuckles over his lower lip. "Not by a long shot."

"Did you...did you love her very much?"

As he looked into Suzanne's eyes, he wondered if he'd ever understood love before. What he'd felt for Amelia, as opposed to the depth of feeling he had for Suzanne, was like comparing a drawing done with crayons to a Rembrandt. Yet he hadn't told Suzanne he loved her, and she hadn't said those words to him.

They would say the words soon, he thought. But they were both being cautious, and that made sense. Feelings this powerful needed to be handled with extreme care.

"I thought I loved her," he said at last. "Maybe I did, as much as any twenty-year-old guy with very little experience in the matter can love a girl. When I dropped out of school, I took a job as a janitor at the college so I could be near her. Of course, that wasn't acceptable. She wanted a college boy, not a janitor."

Suzanne cupped his face in both hands. "What a fool she was."

"I think she was pretty smart. She knew herself. And she did me a favor, because if she hadn't dumped me, I'd be pushing papers right now at some job I hated instead of doing what I love."

"And you really do love it?"

He saw there was no judgment implied by her question, just natural curiosity. "I really do. I used to wonder what my dad saw in the job, but now I know. Every day is different, and I don't have to wear a tie or play office politics. Plus, my mind is free to go over all the things I read at night. Now that I think about it, my dad was a big reader, too. He used to..." Greg paused as he heard a familiar scratching at the bedroom door.

Suzanne lifted her head. "Matilda?"

"Yeah. I'm afraid she's feeling left out."

"Poor kitty. She's used to sharing your bed." Suzanne glanced at the bedside clock. "Good grief. I had no idea it was that late. I need to scurry back upstairs or risk running into some of our early risers."

He sighed. "I hate for you to go."

"I hate to go." She gave him a gentle kiss. "But I need to."

"I guess you're right." He gathered her close and gazed into her eyes. "This has been the best night of my life."

She smiled. "Mine, too. Now let me go, or you know what will happen."

"Nice things."

"Nice things can be postponed until tonight."

Tonight seemed like an eternity to wait, but he knew they both had lives to lead. He had a feeling that tonight, however, would be the magic moment when they each confessed how they felt. "Let's go out to dinner," he said.

"At Jerry's?"

"No, not Jerry's. A quiet place. A romantic place. Somewhere we can dance."

She smiled. "You dance?"

"Uh-huh. Do you?"

"Sort of."

"Sort of is good enough for me. All I really want is a little public foreplay."

She laughed as she wiggled against him. "As if we need that."

"We don't, but it'll be fun. Now stop that, or you'll never get out of this bed and Matilda will scratch a hole in the door while we're otherwise occupied."

"Can't you fix the door?"

"Yep. But I'd rather spend the time with you." He kissed her quickly and released her. "Now's the time for you to go upstairs. And get lots of rest. I have a feeling you won't be sleeping tonight."

SUZANNE LEFT Greg's apartment in a hurry. Before long, some of the other tenants would be stirring, and she wanted to be back in her apartment before then. Perhaps no one would know that she was naked under her coat, but she would know. She was a wilder woman than she had been twenty-four hours ago, but not quite wild enough to carry off waltzing down the hall wearing only a winter coat.

But she hadn't liked having to race away like that, she

thought as she climbed the fire stairs to her floor. Perhaps if she'd been able to leave at a more leisurely pace, one of them would have worked up the courage to speak those three little words. It might even have been her.

She wouldn't mind having Greg say it first, though. Although she was nearly positive that he loved her, she couldn't completely erase the thought that this was all part of his comforting technique. She didn't really believe that, but a trace of doubt remained. A declaration of love on his part would wipe it out.

Still, he might be waiting for her to say something. Even though she'd said that she didn't care how he earned his living, he was obviously sensitive about it and might wonder if she'd be happy with a handyman. Smiling, she thought about how absolutely happy she would be with one particular handyman.

Maybe she needed to be the one to speak first. Tonight would be the perfect chance, now that they had a romantic dinner planned. She wondered if he could afford the kind of place that he'd suggested. Something told her not to question that, though. Someday they might have to deal with the fact that she made more than he did. She didn't care at all, but he might.

They had more to work out, but she believed they'd have no problem doing that. And she'd definitely buy him a Christmas present—something naughty, like body paints or flavored oil, something she would never, ever have had the nerve to buy a man before. Because of Greg, she had the nerve now.

She opened the door to the fire stairs on her floor and peered down the hall, relieved to find it empty. She walked quickly toward her door, and didn't realize she had a problem until she stood facing it.

She'd forgotten to bring a key. She, who never forgot

such things, had forgotten this time. It was sort of funny, that her transformation into a wild woman had caused her to be less anal.

But now she'd have to run back downstairs and get Greg up here to let her in. In the amount of time that would take, someone was liable to come along, which was exactly what she'd been trying to avoid.

Then she had a thought. Maybe she'd not only forgotten a key, but she'd also forgotten to lock the door behind her. In her wild-woman mode, anything was possible. She turned the knob and jiggled it, just in case. No such luck.

With a sigh of resignation, she turned to head back down the hall. Then she heard the click of a lock. Turning back, she stared as the knob turned and the door opened.

A fully dressed but tousled Jared stood in the doorway rubbing sleep from his eyes.

At first she wondered if she could be having a nightmare. Jared didn't live in her apartment anymore. But as she realized that she wasn't dreaming, a sick sense of inevitability settled over her. He'd packed up and left during a big fight, and she'd never talked to him again. Hadn't wanted to, actually.

But Terri, far more worldly than she was, had urged her to have one more conversation with him, just so that she could get her key back. She, coward that she was, hadn't done it. She'd rationalized that Jared had probably thrown it away. Apparently not.

He glanced at his watch, then back at her. "Where the hell have you been all night?"

15

SUZANNE'S FIRST REACTION was to blush and stammer. After all, she was standing in the hallway wearing only her coat and her snow boots. Besides, Jared used to intimidate the heck out of her, and old habits were hard to break.

But damned if she wouldn't break them. She lifted her chin and gave him an icy stare. "Excuse me." Then she walked right past him, through the living room, which she noticed was already cluttered with his stuff, and into her bedroom. She closed the bedroom door and locked it.

"Suzanne!" Angry-sounding footsteps approached the door. "You didn't answer me!"

She took off her coat and boots on her way to the bathroom.

"I've been here since eleven," he called through the door. "I assumed you'd come home sometime, since your suitcases weren't gone. Are you gonna tell me where you've been or not?"

"Not!"

"Damn it, unlock this door." He rattled the knob.

She ignored him, turned on the shower and stepped under the spray. She would have to deal with him sooner or later. For one thing, she needed to get her key back. Either that or change the locks, but that was stupid, considering that changing the locks would cost her money. Greg could do it for her, but she'd rather have Greg do other things for her, things that made better use of his clever hands.

Oh, he had such clever hands. She was reminded of that as she scrubbed her thoroughly satisfied body. Maybe tonight they'd take a shower together and experience making love under the spray. She was considering asking him if he'd like to come up to her place tonight. And bring his condoms.

Just thinking of tonight aroused her all over again. Greg made her feel like the sort of woman who drove men mad with desire, like Cleopatra or Helen of Troy. In his arms she lost all her inhibitions, as evidenced by the red marks on his gorgeous buns. She was glad she hadn't drawn blood with her fingernails. He'd assured her he wouldn't have cared.

Although staying in the shower had considerable appeal, she finally faced the fact that she was hiding in there. She might outwait Jared, but that was the sort of tactic the old Suzanne would have favored. The new Suzanne took decisive action.

So she turned off the shower and stepped out on the fluffy mat. Sure enough, Jared was still carrying on outside her bedroom door.

"...ridiculous to be wandering around Chicago in the middle of the night by yourself. I assume you were by yourself, because nobody walked you to your door. If you were with a guy and he didn't even bother to see you to your door after keeping you out until dawn, then he's a loser."

While Jared raved on about the dangers single women faced on the streets of Chicago, she dressed in a pair of black sweatpants. As she was about to put on the black sweatshirt that matched them, she saw the sweater she'd worn the night before lying across her bed where she'd left it. She picked that up and pulled it over her head.

Then she wandered back to the bathroom and gazed at

herself in the mirror as she wondered whether or not to put on makeup. Although she didn't want to fix herself up for Jared, she didn't want to look young and vulnerable, either. She settled on some mascara, a little blush and some red lipstick.

There. She looked more like a woman to be reckoned with now, especially if she left her hair kind of wild and kinky, which increased her sense of presence. Finally she put on her running shoes, ran her fingers through her hair to make it stand out even more, and walked over to the door.

"It's obvious to me that you need a man in your life," Jared said, his commanding voice only slightly muted by the thickness of the door. "Leave you on your own and you start doing all sorts of crazy things."

Wonderful things, she thought. Taking a deep breath, she opened the door.

"And I—oh, so you finally decided to come out. Your hair's a mess, by the way, and what's with the sweater? I saw it on your bed and figured it was out there because you'd finally decided to give it away. Don't tell me you've taken up skiing. You are so not the skiing type. One trip down the bunny slopes and you'd—"

"Jared, do you think you could shut up for two seconds?"

He stared at her. "What do you mean?"

"I mean shut up. Close your trap. Stuff a sock in it."

He blinked, then narrowed his eyes. "You sound different."

"That's because I *am* different." She studied him and acknowledged that he was a handsome man, but the arrogance in his brown eyes spoiled his dark-haired, movie-star good looks. "Now, what are you doing letting yourself into my apartment at this hour?"

"I came to see you, and you weren't here, so I—"

"Made yourself at home?" She glanced around at the newspapers scattered over her white sofa, the half-eaten sandwich on a plate on the coffee table and the opened Coke can that had left rings on the glass.

She also noticed that her red pillow was lying at the end of the sofa where she'd left it after she and Greg had frolicked there. The thought that Jared had put his head on the same pillow while he waited for her to come home brought a fresh surge of anger. "You certainly did make yourself at home."

"This used to be my home, too," he said quietly.

"In case you hadn't noticed, you moved out six months ago. And funny thing, but now that I'm paying all the rent, I have this crazy idea that the place belongs to me."

"Well, now, it does. It most certainly does." His tone softened and he used that slow, sexy smile that once had made her feel lucky that a man who looked like Jared wanted to be her guy. "And I didn't mean to trespass. I just needed you, honey, so I acted on impulse and came over."

"There's no law against that." She didn't acknowledge his astounding statement that he needed her. She'd have to take time to digest that one. During their relationship he'd never uttered those words. Instead, he'd usually carried on about how much *she* needed *him*. "The problem is that you came in and spent the night here."

"I thought I'd surprise you."

"Oh, you did that."

"And I thought, since you didn't ask for the key back, that you were hoping that one of these days I might show up."

Bingo. She hadn't wanted to admit that to herself, but there was some truth in his assumption. Now that she had more self-confidence, she was embarrassed to think that she'd secretly wanted Jared to come back, despite knowing that he was loud, arrogant and sloppy.

Greg had shown her that she didn't have to settle for Jared. Just in time, too. If she hadn't spent the past three nights with Greg, Jared might have been able to swoop in and bulldoze her again, especially considering that it was the holiday season.

"What do you say, Suzanne?" He stepped closer. "I've missed you. And you know what? Your hair looks kind of sexy like that."

The scent of his aftershave was familiar, but it failed to thrill her the way it used to. She backed up. "It's too late, Jared."

"I can't believe that. I've been an idiot not to realize how great we were together, but I can see that now. It's Christmas, honey. Let's find a sprig of mistletoe and make up. I think it's time you and I started talking about what kind of wedding we'd like."

She stepped back again before he could reach for her. "I'm afraid not, Jared."

His look of amazement was followed by a scowl. "There's someone else, isn't there?"

"As a matter of fact, there is."

His scowl darkened. "Who is he?"

"That's my business."

"I saw how bedraggled you looked when you came in here, with your hair going every which way. You were with him, weren't you?"

"I don't have to answer your questions, Jared. Come to think of it, you've overstayed your welcome." She held out her hand. "I'd like my key back."

He ignored her. "If he's the kind who left you to find your own way home, then you'd better reconsider, babe.

It's not every day that a guy like me comes along and makes you an offer."

"There's no doubt you're one of a kind." She wondered how she'd ever considered this pompous fool as a marriage prospect. If he'd proposed six months ago, she would have accepted. The thought made her shiver.

"You're damn right. So let's forget this nonsense and get back together."

"The key, Jared." She stuck her hand out again.

He fished in his pocket and pulled it out. But as he put it in her hand, he grabbed her wrist and pulled her roughly into his arms.

"Jared, stop it!" She struggled to get away.

"Come on, Suzanne." He held her tight. "You've forgotten how good it could be between us."

"Ha. It wasn't that good, as you always reminded me. Now let me go." She regretted not starting at the gym a few months ago, so she'd be stronger. He, on the other hand, was plenty strong.

"Nope." He managed to get hold of her chin and lowered his head.

"I'll bite you."

He didn't look the least worried. "That's not your style and you know it." He covered her mouth with his and thrust his tongue inside.

She made good on her promise.

Yelping, he leaped backward. "You really did bite me!" He stuck his tongue out and wiped it with his finger. "I'm bleeding!"

"It was either that or knee you in the balls. I thought you might prefer the bite."

"Suzanne, you've gone wacko. I—"

The doorbell buzzed.

Suzanne started toward it with a sigh. "Now see what

you've done. With all your carrying on, you've disturbed one of my neighbors." She opened the door, ready to apologize, and faced Greg.

As he stared at her, his smile faded. "I, um, came up because I—"

"Suzanne? Who is it, honey?"

She cringed.

Greg's eyes narrowed. "Is Jared here?"

"Yes, but—"

Jared came up behind her. "Hey, I know you. You're the handyman guy. Suzanne was just in the shower. Did the apartment below report a leak or something?"

Suzanne stood there in an agony of indecision. She didn't think it would be a good idea to let Jared know that Greg was the man she'd been involved with. For one thing, Greg might not appreciate that. They'd shared so much, but they hadn't talked about where they were going from here. She thought she knew, but she wasn't sure enough to go public, especially in front of Jared, a man she didn't want to know her personal business.

But she didn't want Greg to think what he was obviously thinking, seeing Jared here at this hour of the morning. Then she noticed Greg staring at her mouth, and remembered that her lipstick was probably smeared. Worse yet, she didn't have to look to know that Jared would be wearing some of it, too.

Greg's gaze was bleak. "Actually, I made a mistake. The tenant in 46B asked me to come up this morning and check a light switch. I'm off by a floor. Sorry to have bothered you."

Finally Suzanne had an inspiration. "Listen, as long as you're here, the pipe under my bathroom sink has been giving me problems again. When you're finished in 46B, I'd appreciate it if you'd stop back by and check it out."

"Unfortunately I can't do it today," Greg said. "Put something under it to catch the drip and I'll try to get to it next week."

She panicked. Although she'd straighten this out eventually, she didn't want Greg to go any longer than necessary with the wrong impression. "It's a terrible leak," she said.

Greg looked into her eyes. "In that case, maybe you should have Jared take a look at it."

She was desperate to get him to come back. "He doesn't know anything about plumbing."

"Hey," Jared said. "I know enough to check a leak. I'll—"

"See?" Greg said. "You'll be fine." Then he turned and walked away.

She wanted to call him back, but now wasn't the time to stage a scene. She closed the door and realized she had the key still clutched in her hand.

Fury boiling in her, she stalked over to the sofa where Jared had tossed his coat. Snatching it up, she threw it at him. "Get out of here," she said in a tightly controlled voice. "Get out of here right now or I'm calling the cops."

"You *are* getting weird."

"Too weird for you. Now, are you leaving, or shall I dial 911?"

"I'm leaving." He touched his wounded tongue gingerly with his finger. "You've changed, Suzanne. You've definitely changed. The way you are now, I wouldn't want you."

"No, I don't believe you would. Goodbye, Jared."

Shaking his head, he opened the door. "Man, have you changed." Then he walked out and closed the door behind him.

She ran over and locked it before hurrying back to the

phone. After dialing Greg's number, she paced, waiting for him to pick up. She got his machine and wondered if he was there, listening to her urgent message.

Hanging up the phone after begging him to call her, she unlocked her door and went out into the hall, making sure she had the key this time. She charged down the fire stairs to the basement. Then she rang his doorbell. And rang it some more. Damn. Apparently he'd left the building entirely.

Well, he couldn't hide from her forever. Eventually she'd get in touch with him and let him know that Jared's presence there hadn't been at all the way it had looked. Then she headed for Terri's apartment.

Terri came to the door in a nightshirt that had Buffy the Vampire Slayer on the front. She rubbed her eyes and stared at Suzanne. "That's some sweater you got there, chick. Especially this early on a Saturday morning."

"Sorry about this, but I have to talk to you."

"Obviously." She backed away from the door. "Come on. I'll make us some coffee."

Terri's place was the same floor plan as Suzanne's, but there the resemblance ended. Terri loved trendy colors, and right now she was into sage and lavender. Her walls were filled with motivational posters. Although she wasn't messy, her apartment always looked a little cluttered because of all the souvenirs she'd collected while attending sales meetings around the country.

Suzanne followed her into the kitchen. "It's about Greg."

"I figured." Terri loaded coffee into a gold mesh filter.

"I'm in love with him."

Terri spilled the water she'd been pouring into the coffeemaker. Then she swore and glanced over at Suzanne. "You think you are, sweetie, but—"

"I don't just think. I know. And he's in love with me. I think."

"Ho, boy." Terri started the coffee and turned back to Suzanne, her eyes full of sympathy. "But he didn't say he was in love with you, did he?"

"Not exactly." Suzanne fought panic. "But I think he was planning to, tonight. Except now he thinks I'm back with Jared."

"Okay. Let's start over. Tell me everything, from the beginning."

Suzanne gave Terri an overview, but she wasn't about to tell her friend the details of her lovemaking with Greg. She did, however, mention that he'd taken her to Jerry's, and that they'd spent most of the night together after that.

"I think he's treating me differently from the others," she said. "I think he's told me things about himself that he didn't tell everyone."

Instead of responding, Terri got out mugs and poured them each a cup of coffee. "Let's take this into the living room," she said, handing Suzanne a mug.

Carrying her mug, Suzanne followed her and perched on the end of Terri's sage-green couch. "You think I'm setting myself up for a fall, don't you?"

Terri gazed at her with a sad expression. "If he's the kind of bachelor type I've been led to believe, I can't see why he'd give that up all of a sudden."

"Because he's found the one he wants!"

"I guess that's always possible, but unless he's said so..." Terri shook her head. "You can track him down and explain about Jared if you want, and maybe that will buy you a little more time. He probably saw you with Jared and figured his services were no longer required. The thing is, eventually that will happen, anyway, so breaking it off now might be less awkward."

Suzanne clutched the mug in both hands. "I can't leave it like this between us. I have to talk to him and explain that I didn't rush straight from him back to Jared."

"But that's how it's supposed to work." Terri sipped her coffee. "Not that you get Jared back, necessarily, but that you're ready to move on to someone new. That's what a rebound man is all about."

"I don't want anybody new. Or old." The lack of sleep and worry about Greg had frayed her nerves to the point that tears were not far away. "I don't want anybody except Greg. And I think he wants me."

Terri seemed to contemplate that as she took another long swallow of coffee. "You left him a message on his machine, right?"

"Right."

"Then that's all you can do. If he feels the way you think he does, he'll respond to that message."

Suzanne wasn't so sure. After knowing how Amelia had hurt him years ago, she wondered if he'd take the chance that it would happen again.

"You know, he might have called you already," Terri suggested gently.

She was right, Suzanne thought, and she wouldn't get the call sitting here. "I need to go check my messages." She stood. "I'll pour my coffee back in the pot. I didn't drink any of it."

Terri waved her hand. "Leave it, leave it. Just go."

She put her mug down. "Thanks for listening."

"Anytime. And let me know if you hear from him."

"I will. I most certainly will." Then she left Terri's and hurried back to her apartment. No message waited for her on her answering machine. But it was early yet. Greg cared about her. She had to believe that he would call.

GREG WALKED the snowy streets of downtown Chicago. At first he'd been practically alone, but as the morning wore on, the sidewalks filled with Christmas shoppers. Greg hoped his foul mood wasn't catching. The way he felt, he might be capable of sucking the Christmas spirit right out of these happy crowds of people.

He picked up some black coffee to go from a little shop on Michigan Avenue and sipped it through the slit in the plastic top as he continued to walk. The coffee tasted as bitter as he felt. He couldn't believe that he'd been such a fool as to think that Suzanne would be happy with a handyman instead of some corporate type.

How Jared had ended up at her apartment so damn fast, within an hour of her leaving Greg's bed, was a mystery, but it didn't really matter. Jared had been there, with Suzanne's lipstick smeared all over his face, and that was all Greg had needed to see.

Obviously Suzanne had been upset that he'd caught her with Jared, and he was sure she'd want to talk with him and make some excuse about it. He didn't have the time. From now on, he was steering clear of women like Suzanne. Unless he planned to get a college degree and a corner office, he was doomed to fail with them.

The memory of making love to Suzanne and feeling as if he held the keys to the universe hovered on the edge of his mind, but he pushed it firmly away. He couldn't afford to keep memories like that. They hurt too much. And besides, they were a lie.

He had a problem, though, and that's why he was walking out here on a cold Saturday morning. He'd made the mistake of letting Suzanne into his apartment, so now the place was filled with images of her. Even his cat was tainted. He'd have to go back sometime today, if for no other reason than to check on Matilda. But he was dreading it.

Deep down, he knew that letting Suzanne into his apartment hadn't been his biggest mistake. His biggest mistake, one that might haunt him forever, was letting her into his heart.

16

WHEN GREG DIDN'T call her back all weekend, Suzanne went down to the basement Sunday night and rang his doorbell. No answer. She rang it twice more and waited. Still no answer. Returning to her apartment, she called and left another message. This was not going well.

All week she kept hoping she'd accidentally run into him. It had happened enough times in the past to kick start her fantasy life, but now that he was more than a fantasy, she never saw him. Apparently he could make himself scarce if he wanted to. Terri kept suggesting gently that Suzanne should let the whole thing go.

But she couldn't. Whether she was someone special to Greg or just another notch in his tool belt, she couldn't let their last interaction be that sleazy scene at her apartment door. She wanted Greg to think well of her, and right now he had the wrong image.

By December twenty-third, her frustration at not being able to talk to Greg had reached a fever pitch. The next day she was scheduled to take the train to her mother's house in Moline for a two-day holiday break, giving her too much time to think. She simply *had* to clear the air with Greg, not only to explain about Jared's surprise visit, but also to get some answers for herself.

Although Terri hadn't been to bed with him, apparently Jennifer had. Suzanne needed to know if there had been the same deep feeling of connection in Jennifer's case. If there had been, it would be a terrible blow, but Suzanne decided she'd rather know than remain in limbo. If Jennifer's experience had been similar to hers, then she'd do her best to forget Greg and get on with her life.

She called Jennifer at work and arranged to meet her for lunch at the Cheesecake Factory. She needed to buy a cheesecake to take to her mother for Christmas, anyway. If the news from Jennifer was really bad, Suzanne would buy two cheesecakes—one for her mother and one for her to devour tonight while she cried.

Jennifer arrived at the restaurant looking as fashionable as ever, from her trendy dress to her leather trench coat. As Jennifer approached the table, Suzanne wondered if she had the guts to go through with this. Looking at Jennifer and imagining her in bed with Greg was already mental torture. If Greg had said and done the same tender, sexy things with Jennifer as he had with Suzanne, a whole restaurant full of cheesecakes wouldn't be enough to ease the pain.

Suzanne had to work up to the main topic, so she was happy to chitchat about Christmas plans until their sandwiches arrived. Finally she realized they were running out of time. Pushing aside her plate, she took another sip of coffee and noticed her hand was shaking.

She put down the coffee and cleared her throat. "Jennifer, I don't want to pry into your personal life, but I know you spent some time with Greg, and it's very important to me to know—"

"Oh, *Greg*."

Suzanne looked into her shining eyes and her heart sank. "You, um, got along well with him?"

"Absolutely. He's such a wonderful guy. He made me feel…like a desirable woman again."

A lump clogged Suzanne's throat. He'd done the same for her. "I can't imagine you ever not feeling that way."

"Are you kidding? Getting dumped by a guy, especially if you really liked him, can sabotage anybody's self-confidence. Don't you read the scab sheets? If Meg Ryan can get depressed, then think how vulnerable the rest of us are."

"Right." Suzanne forced herself to sound positive. "And that's where a rebound man like Greg comes in handy." She even managed a tiny laugh. "I mean, I was so repressed, sexually. Greg took care of that in no time. What a guy."

"Yeah."

Now that she'd broached the subject, she discovered that she couldn't leave it alone. "That massage he gives is really something. It really blew me away."

"Mmm."

She might as well know the worst. Lowering her voice, she looked directly into Jennifer's dark eyes. "I have to ask you this. Did you feel an almost...well, a sort of spiritual connection when you...made love to him?"

"Uh..."

"Look, I realize this is very personal, and we don't know each other all that well, but I...I need to know."

The longer Jennifer hesitated, the louder Suzanne's heart beat. It sounded like the drumroll as a condemned prisoner faced a firing squad, which summed up the way Suzanne felt.

At last Jennifer blew out a breath. "Can I trust you not to say a word about this to anyone?"

"Of course." Suzanne clenched her hands together on the table.

"I didn't sleep with him."

Suzanne blinked. "You *didn't*? But I thought—"

"I didn't want to be the one he didn't sleep with, so I let on that I had."

Dazed by this unexpected information, Suzanne tried to figure out what was going on. It was exactly the same story Terri had told her. A thought came to her, flashing like a diamond in a pile of sawdust. What if *nobody* had slept with Greg?

"You won't tell anyone about this?" Jennifer said.

"No. You can trust me."

"He's such a hunk, and I would have loved to go to bed with him, but all we did was talk. Maybe that was for the best, because the relationship couldn't have gone anywhere, with him being the handyman and all." She paused and gazed at Suzanne. "I envy you the experience. I take it he was...good?"

"Mmm." Now it was Suzanne's turn to be evasive.

"What a fantasy, to have a brief affair with somebody like that, knowing you'll never marry him, so that it becomes this perfect little jewel of a memory to tuck away."

Suzanne started to argue the point, but she quickly realized that a woman with Jennifer's mind-set wouldn't understand why Suzanne thought marrying Greg, no matter what his job, would be a privilege. No wonder Greg had been sensitive about this. He'd run into several women who thought being a handyman was an unacceptable job for their future husband. Oh, well. Their loss.

She and Jennifer said their goodbyes and both left with boxes of cheesecake. Suzanne bought an extra one, even though the news from Jennifer had been surprisingly good. Maybe, just maybe, an occasion would arise that would demand a celebration. Chocolate-fudge cheesecake would certainly do the trick.

That evening she tried Greg again, just because it had become almost a habit now, not because she expected to get an answer. Sure enough, his machine came on. "I'm leaving for Moline tomorrow," she said. "I won't be back until late Christmas night, so I wanted to wish you a merry Christmas."

Then she paid a visit to Carolyn's apartment. Fortunately she was home, and although it took some skillful conversation on Suzanne's part, eventually Carolyn admitted that she hadn't slept with Greg, either. Suzanne's theory was sounding better and better, but she had no more leads and no more time to check them, anyway.

Besides, she had enough evidence to show that Greg didn't treat every woman the way he'd treated her. That seemed like enough to warrant giving Mr. Greg Stone the third degree about his original intentions toward her. There had to be a way to get him to come out of hiding. She had a train ride to Moline tomorrow and a train ride back on Christmas Day. That would be enough thinking time to plan how to do it.

GREG LOVED being home with his family on Christmas, especially now that the merriment had returned to the household. They had great fun opening presents on Christmas morning, and everyone pitched in to help with the huge meal that followed late that afternoon.

Normally Greg stayed on into the evening playing board games or even a few rounds of poker. But as darkness fell, he grew restless and eager to get back to his apartment. He told himself it was so that Matilda wouldn't be alone too long, but he knew she'd be fine. He'd left her plenty of food and water to carry her through the two days and one night he'd planned to be gone.

It wasn't Matilda who drew him back to Chicago. It was Suzanne. She'd been far more persistent than he'd expected, and she was wearing him down. He'd just about decided that he might have to see her, after all. After Christmas, he'd told himself. After Christmas he'd call her and arrange a meeting, maybe at some neutral spot like a coffee shop, where he wouldn't be tempted to do or say anything dumb.

But then she'd called to wish him a merry Christmas, and there had been something different in her voice. He couldn't put his finger on it, but somehow he expected...something to happen. She'd said she wouldn't be back until late tonight, so it was stupid of him to leave his family on the chance she'd come in earlier.

But he did it anyway. When he walked into his apartment, Matilda meowed and made a pest of herself until he gave her a little bit of the turkey his mother had insisted he take home. He glanced at his answering-machine light, hoping it would be blinking with a new message from Suzanne. It wasn't.

So, he'd been a fool to race back here on the strength of that little note of excitement or anticipation he'd heard in her voice two nights ago. It might have been nothing more than her eagerness to spend a couple of days with her mom. Even so, on impulse, he turned off his machine for the night. If she called, and she probably wouldn't, he would talk to her.

Talk to her, ha. You'll go up to her apartment if she asks you to. Yeah, he probably would. Damn it, he wanted to see her. Even if seeing her was a bad idea he'd live to regret, he wanted to give it a try. She'd wished him Merry Christmas, and he hadn't returned the sentiment. It would be Christmas for a few more hours.

Picking up his mother's gift—a leather-bound volume of classic love poems—he sat in his chair and began thumbing through it. His mother had always known what a sentimental sap he was. Every time he went home, she found a moment to draw him aside and ask if he'd found anybody "special."

The question had been harder to answer this Christmas. And the more he'd evaded, the more she'd suspected. When he'd left early, his mother had waved goodbye with a knowing expression. He'd never been any good at fooling his mother.

Matilda joined him in the chair, so he read her something by Elizabeth Barrett Browning, which made her purr. But she seemed equally happy with one of Shakespeare's sonnets, so apparently she had a wide area of appreciation. As for him, he couldn't read any of it without thinking of Suzanne—her eyes, her lips, her hair, her breasts, the wonder of sinking inside her, the joy of making her cry out with pleasure.

If only he hadn't gone to her apartment to ask her out for breakfast, he wouldn't have found her with Jared, both of them wearing incriminating lipstick smears. That picture kept superimposing itself over the others that he carried in his mental wallet.

When the phone rang, his pulse ratcheted up several more beats per minute. Matilda leaped from the chair, but he took his time getting up. All the while he told himself this was probably a tenant with a problem, and probably not the tenant he wanted to hear from tonight.

He picked up the receiver. "Hello?"

"Greg!"

He felt light-headed. It was her. Incredibly, it was her. "I thought you weren't coming back until later."

"I took an earlier train, and thank God I did. I have a major leak up here, Greg. I'm talking major. I didn't expect to get you, but I thought I'd try, anyway. If you hadn't been home, I was going to have to look for a twenty-four-hour emergency service, although I doubt *anybody* is working on Christmas night."

"Probably not." His brain whirled as he wondered if she really had a leak or not. If she really had one, then this call was just what it seemed. In fact, wonderful Jared, the guy who didn't do plumbing, might be there with her. If he was, that would clinch things forever and ever.

"I hate to bother you on Christmas, but can you come up and take a look?"

"Yeah, I can come up." He tried to sound bored with the idea, but although the words were the right ones, his tone probably gave him away.

"Great. See you soon."

He left so fast he forgot his toolbox. Halfway to the third floor he remembered it and had to go down again. On the way back up he made those metal fire stairs sing. He was pumped. He was ready. If Jared was there, he'd fix the damn pipe and then he'd tell Ms. Suzanne Talbot what he thought of her.

If Jared wasn't there, he'd...well, he'd figure that out when the time came. His heart was racing and he was breathing hard by the time he rang her doorbell. He took a deep breath, and wiped one sweaty palm on his jeans. Pumped was one thing, but frazzled and panting would not be cool.

She threw open the door, and she'd never looked more beautiful to him. Her cheeks were flushed, her hair was loose and sexy, her feet were bare and she wore the cutest Christmas sweatshirt with angels all over it. The sweatshirt was splotched with water, but that didn't spoil the look of it. If he hadn't been holding the toolbox he might not have been able to resist grabbing her and kissing her. He gripped the toolbox and told himself to stay calm.

"I thought you'd never get here," she said.

"Is it the bathroom sink again?"

"Yes. Those little lines that go to the faucet, you know? One's broken, and I don't know how to turn off the water, and it's squirting everywhere."

"Broken?" He frowned as he walked into the apartment and headed back toward her bedroom. Nothing had been wrong with that copper tubing when he'd been under there a few weeks ago.

"Broken." She followed him.

He took the time to glance around and saw no sign of Jared. He'd expect the jerk to be hanging around if he and Suzanne were back together. After all, it was Christmas. Maybe he was in the bathroom holding his finger against the leak, acting like some macho hero. In that case, Greg thought, he'd pretend that he needed to go back downstairs and get some other part before he could do anything, just so Jared had to stay in a cramped position a while longer.

Jared wasn't in the bathroom, but sure enough, water was spraying out from under the sink. The place was a mess.

"See? I wasn't kidding, was I?"

"Nope." Greg waded in, getting himself soaked in the process. He crawled under the sink and turned off the water. Then he wiped the water from his eyes and peered at the line. Unless he was hallucinating, somebody had taken a hammer and chisel to it.

He eased himself out from under the sink and stood. Pulling a towel from a nearby rack, he dried his face.

"Can you fix it?" she asked.

He hung the towel back where he'd found it. "Yeah," he said. "I can fix it."

"Thank goodness."

He nudged off one sneaker and stepped over the wet

floor to the dry carpeting of her bedroom. Then he repeated the process with the other shoe. "The question is," he said, turning to her, "why did you break it?"

She took a breath and looked ready to deny it.

"I know you broke it, Suzanne. Just tell me why."

She let out her breath slowly. "Because I had to see you, and you seemed determined to avoid me. I went over to my dad's today and borrowed a plumbing-repair book, so I had some idea how to do it."

"You went over to your dad's? I thought you were afraid to do that and get your mother upset."

"I was, but Mom and I worked that out."

"Good." He was happy for her. Even if they weren't destined to be together, he wanted her to have a nice life.

She smiled. "Yeah, it was a good thing. I spent Christmas Eve with Mom and Christmas morning with Dad and his family." She pulled the front of the sweatshirt away from her body. "They gave me this."

"I like it. Even wet, it looks good." He thought it would look good lying on the floor, too, but that was getting way ahead of the game. "So, did Jared go with you down to your mom's?"

Her eyes darkened. "That's what I had to talk to you about. Jared came over uninvited that night."

"Really? You sure looked happy to see him."

"You mean the lipstick."

"I mean the lipstick, and the fact that you showered while he was here, and come to think of it, he was sort of rumpled up, like he'd been involved in some fun and games."

"I came home and found him in the apartment, and—"

"He still had a key?" No matter how much Greg wanted this story to come out right, he wouldn't be taken for a fool.

"Yes, and that was my fault. I should have asked him for

it months ago, but I didn't, because until I became involved with you, part of me must have wanted him back."

Greg's heart wrenched. "You know what? I don't need to hear this. In fact, use your kitchen sink for a few days. I'll fix this while you're at work." He reached for his toolbox.

"Wait!" She grabbed his arm. "Didn't you hear me? I said *until I became involved with you*. You helped me see that Jared is all wrong for me, that I can do better than that."

He sighed. At least he'd been good for something. "I take it you discovered that when you kissed him."

"I didn't kiss him. He kissed me, and I bit his tongue."

He stared at her. "You did what?"

"I bit his tongue. I told him he was lucky I didn't knee him in the balls."

In spite of his heavy heart, he had to smile. "Congratulations. Sounds like you're going to be fine, Suzanne. I'm glad I could be of service." He glanced down to where she was clutching his arm. "So now you've told me how it was, and I'm happy for you. You can let me go now."

"Not yet."

He looked into her eyes. "Suzanne, it's better if we—"

"I did some checking, and now I know you didn't sleep with *all* the women you've dealt with in this apartment building."

He stared at her in confusion. "What in hell are you talking about?"

"When Terri first told me about you, she implied that you cheered up women who'd been dumped by taking them to bed."

"*What?*"

"Then Terri finally admitted that she hadn't slept with you, but she figured everyone else had. Now I know of two others you didn't sleep with, so—"

"I haven't slept with *any* of them!" he roared. "I can't believe this! Are you telling me I have a reputation for being some kind of...of...*gigolo?*" He was so upset he could barely think, let alone talk. All along he'd thought he was acting as an unpaid psychologist, and these damn women had been saying that he'd *slept with them?* It was too much.

"You haven't?" For some strange reason her face had begun to glow and she had a huge smile on her face. "You mean I'm the only one?"

"Of course you're the only one!"

"Greg, you're really red in the face. Maybe you should sit down or something."

"I'm not going to sit down, I'm going to pay a visit to every damn one of those women and tell them what I think of their—"

"You can't."

"What do you mean, I can't? I most certainly can."

"They told me this in confidence. If you confront them, they'll know that I blabbed to you."

He was having a very hard time making sense of this. "Which makes no difference, since I'm the one who's supposed to have been treating this apartment building like some damn harem! Since I'm the last to know, I think I have a right to ask what the hell they think they're doing, dragging my reputation through the mud like that."

She took a firmer hold on his arm. "Not through the mud. They rave about your abilities." She blushed. "I expected you'd blow me away with your expertise, and you did. I thought it was because you'd had so much practice."

"It was because I loved you!" Too late he realized what he'd said. He stood there staring at her, knowing there was no taking it back. "But don't worry about that. I'll get over it. I—"

"You will?" The light faded from her eyes. "How can

you get over something like what we've shared? I'm sure I won't."

He went still. Then his heart began hammering triple time. "You won't?"

Her voice was soft, her eyes misty. "Nope. That's really what I wanted to tell you. I love you, Greg. Even when I thought you might have gone to bed with a bunch of other women, I hoped that this time with me was special."

He searched her eyes and found everything he needed to last him a lifetime. Then he scooped her into his arms and showered her with kisses. "You can't even begin to know how special. But I was afraid to hope that you'd want a handyman."

She wound her arms around his neck and kissed him back. "Of course I do. How else will I get my sink fixed?"

He couldn't stop kissing her. "I can fix anything you need repaired."

"Then you'd better do something about my heart. It's beating something fierce."

"That could become a chronic problem." He lifted her in his arms and carried her the short distance to the bed. "I think I need to assess the situation right now."

"Me, too." She smiled up at him. "And I'm convinced I'll need regular maintenance, like for about the next seventy years or so."

He rolled on top of her. "Are you proposing to me?"

"Yes. Will you marry me?"

He gazed at her in wonder. "Absolutely. The sooner the better." He leaned down and feathered her lips with his. "Merry Christmas, sweetheart."

"Oh!" She looked suddenly stricken. "I didn't get you anything."

He grinned. "Oh, I think you did." He slipped his hand under her sweatshirt. "And I can hardly wait to unwrap what you're going to give me."

Epilogue

A year later

SUZANNE CUDDLED next to Greg on the sofa and gazed at the crackling fire while Christmas carols played softly in the background. "I feel sort of selfish, stealing away up here for Christmas instead of spending it with our families," she said.

Greg pulled her closer. "Too late. It's snowing like crazy and the roads would be dangerous, so we can't leave even if we wanted to."

"And Matilda. Don't you feel guilty leaving her for a week?"

"Ha. I swear that cat had something to do with picking out our new apartment. She must have known there was a cat lover right next door. Personally, I think Matilda can hardly wait for us to skip town."

"Mrs. Tuttle does spoil her rotten. She's getting fat." Suzanne nestled her head against Greg's shoulder and enjoyed the mingled scents of the Christmas tree and the fire. "Okay, you've convinced me that we need to be here, after all. It might be our last chance to be alone on Christmas, anyway." She glanced at him to see if he'd picked up on her hint.

Apparently he'd missed it. "Probably not," he said. "But you don't buy a cottage in Wisconsin unless you're going to use it. That's wasteful. Besides, we'll please them all next Christmas. This year we deserve to please ourselves."

She drew back far enough to look into his eyes. "You'll have to speak for yourself, but as for me, I've been *extremely* pleased."

He looked proud of himself. "You like the flavored body paints Santa brought you?"

"I do. I think I should have been an art major."

He grinned. "Me, too. In fact, maybe we should see how they work while we're lying naked in front of the fire."

"Sounds good." She looked into his eyes, her heart bursting with the Christmas secret she'd been saving until now. She'd decided to reveal it at exactly the same time that she'd proposed and he'd accepted, one year ago. Her sense of drama had sharpened considerably in Greg's company.

His grin widened. "You're up to something."

"Yes." She felt giddy with happiness. "Do you realize it was exactly this time of night last year that I called you up to my apartment to fix the pipe I'd smashed?"

He glanced at the grandfather clock in the corner of their little cottage. "Yeah, I guess it was."

"Well, I have one more present to give you."

His eyes glowed with interest. "Does this require stripping down? I love presents that require stripping down."

"Actually, no. We can strip down later. For now, I just want you to sit there while I go get it."

"Aha. You're going to strip down and come out in one of those sexy outfits you've been collecting."

"No, not exactly." She left the sofa, unable to stand the suspense another minute. "Now stay right there." Hurrying into the bedroom, she undressed quickly and pulled on the new outfit she'd bought a week ago. Then she paraded out and stood in front of him.

He looked confused. "Honey, you'd look sexy in a gunnysack, but I have to tell you, that's what that jumper looks like. It's a nice color, but it doesn't fit you very well."

"It will." She waited for him to figure it out.

"It will?" He frowned. Then, slowly, his frown disappeared and a look of wonder took its place. "It *will?*"

She nodded.

"Omigod." He leaped up and swept her into a bear hug. "Omigod, omigod!"

She couldn't stop laughing. "Do you like your present?"

He looked down at her, his eyes bright. "Yeah," he said, his voice rough with emotion. "I love my present."

"That's good, because you know who's going to be taking care of the little tyke when I'm at the office."

He ran his fingers through her hair. "I can hardly wait." Then he rested his hand against her belly. "Really?"

"Really. I've been dying to tell you, but I wanted to make it part of our first Christmas together. Merry Christmas, my love."

He held her close and cupped her face in one hand. His voice was husky. "A moment ago, when we were snuggling on the sofa, I thought my life couldn't be more perfect. I was wrong. Now it's perfect."

She wound her arms around his neck. "But it really will be the last Christmas we'll be alone for a long, long time."

"Then we'd better make the most of it. Actually, I have one more present for you, too." He reached into the breast pocket of his flannel shirt and pulled out a plastic sprig of mistletoe. "Remember this?"

"You saved it all this time?"

"Yeah." He smiled. "I've been keeping it in my toolbox, sort of like a lucky charm, but I decided to bring it up here this week." He brushed it over her nose. "On the chance that you'd like to get mistletoed."

She gazed up at him and the magic began again, as it always did when she was in his arms. As it always would. She smiled at him, her heart full, while her favorite "Carol of the Bells" began to play. She took it as a sign.

"Mistletoe me," she whispered.

CALL THE ONES YOU LOVE OVER THE HOLIDAYS!

Save $25 off future book purchases when you buy any four Harlequin® or Silhouette® books in October, November and December 2001,

PLUS

receive a phone card good for 15 minutes of long-distance calls to anyone you want in North America!

WHAT AN INCREDIBLE DEAL!

Just fill out this form and attach 4 proofs of purchase (cash register receipts) from October, November and December 2001 books, and Harlequin Books will send you a coupon booklet worth a total savings of $25 off future purchases of Harlequin® and Silhouette® books, AND a 15-minute phone card to call the ones you love, anywhere in North America.

Please send this form, along with your cash register receipts as proofs of purchase, to:
In the USA: Harlequin Books, P.O. Box 9057, Buffalo, NY 14269-9057
In Canada: Harlequin Books, P.O. Box 622, Fort Erie, Ontario L2A 5X3
Cash register receipts must be dated no later than December 31, 2001.
Limit of 1 coupon booklet and phone card per household.
Please allow 4-6 weeks for delivery.

**I accept your offer! Enclosed are 4 proofs of purchase.
Please send me my coupon booklet
and a 15-minute phone card:**

Name: _____

Address: _____ City: _____

State/Prov.: _____ Zip/Postal Code: _____

Account Number (if available): _____

---

097 KJB DAGL
PHQ4013

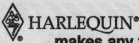

If you enjoyed what you just read,
then we've got an offer you can't resist!

Take 2 bestselling
love stories FREE!
Plus get a FREE surprise gift!